WIVES AT WAR
AND OTHER STORIES

by

Flora Nwapa

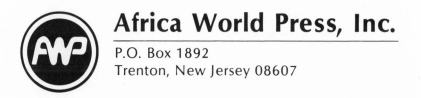

Africa World Press, Inc.

P.O. Box 1892
Trenton, New Jersey 08607

ABOUT THE AUTHOR

Flora Nwapa is Nigeria's first woman novelist, author of the highly praised *Efuru, Idu, This is Lagos and Other Stories, Never Again* and *One is Enough.*

Africa World Press, Inc.
P.O. Box 1892
Trenton, New Jersey 08607

First published in Nigeria by TANA PRESS, 1980

First Africa World Press edition 1992

Cover design and illustration: Ife Designs

Library of Congress Catalog Card Number:
ISBN: 0-86543-
       0-86543-

For my husband Gogo,
whose generosity made the establishment of
Tana Press Limited possible.

041600

CONTENTS

WIVES AT WAR

Ebo and Bisi met at their work place in Lagos. Ebo was the personnel officer in a large multi-national company and Bisi the secretary to the managing director of the company. Ebo was Igbo and Bisi, Yoruba. They saw each other for two years and decided to get married. There was opposition from both families, so they married quietly in the Registry Office.

The marriage was blessed by three sons in quick succession. Bisi was a devoted wife, who was determined to prove that an inter-tribal marriage could and would work. Ebo was also a good husband who did all in his power to see that his family was well provided for. They lived happily, until the coup of January 15th, 1966, which changed everything.

Ebo and his family were obliged to leave Lagos for his home town, Onitsha. Bisi had never visited Onitsha before. Their children spoke only English and Yoruba and no Igbo. But Bisi was determined, like all the other Igbos in Lagos, to make her home at Onitsha, when she saw that her husband was bent on going back home.

At Onitsha, Ebo's uncle provided them with a two bedroom house and a small kitchen. Ebo then travelled to Enugu to see what job he could do to help 'win the war' for Biafra. He got a place in the Ministry of Information in the propaganda section. Ebo soon discovered that the people were being prepared for a long-drawn war and became apprehensive. He decided it was safer to move his

1

family to Port Harcourt where he got a good bungalow in the Shell camp. He travelled to Port Harcourt from Enugu every weekend. Soon Enugu fell, followed quickly by Onitsha and the Government moved to Umuahia. Ebo then moved to the Department of Military Intelligence, known as D.M.I., and was transferred to Port Harcourt.

But the war was not going well for Biafra, and Ebo was determined to keep his family safe and intact. What was he going to tell Bisi's mother if Bisi died or something dreadful happened to her? So he got a map of Eastern Nigeria, studied it very carefully, picked out a village in the Igbo heartland where he would move his family until the end came.

He did not waste time. With the help of his driver, who was from Orlu, at the heart of Igbo land, Ebo got an unfinished concrete house in Okporo village. He offered to roof it with zinc and the landlord readily agreed. But the landlord wondered how a man from the D.M.I. could, in war time, roof a house when millions starved.

Ebo roofed the place and furnished it. Then he brought down some of his army officer friends with their girlfriends for a kind of house warming party. They had a wonderful time and agreed to repeat the occasion.

But the landlord was worried because the villagers had already started calling him a saboteur. He protested, but the word had stuck to him and there was nothing he could do about it other than go into hiding.

This action convinced the villagers that the landlord was indeed a saboteur, so they organised a show down with the 'saboteur' tenants. The night they chose to burn down the house was the night that Ebo brought another group of army officers in His Excellency's Brigade to make merry after a successful "operation".

The villagers came out with their crude weapons, ignorant of the presence of the officers. They tried to break down the house and the officers retaliated. It was a swift and easy operation; the officers rounded the villagers up, and gave them a thorough beating. Those who "resisted arrest" were detained and later carried off to Umuahia.

A week later, Ebo finally brought his family to Okporo. Bisi was completely shattered because of the shellings in Bonny sector. When she heard of the incident between the officers and the villagers, she refused to live in the house for fear of attack by the villagers when her husband was away. But there was no other place for her to go. Ebo told her so. She flared up.

'You, you are wicked, to bring me to this God-forsaken place. There is no food here, there is no water either. You and your uncouth army officers, you . . .'

'Please, Bisi, please see reason. You have to stay here with the children. Nothing will happen to you here. You are well protected, and . . .'

'Protected? By whom? The people are hostile to us. They will poison us, they will kill us. You and your people, you and your propaganda. You told me the war would end in two weeks. And . . .'

'I did not say that.'

'Liar, you are a liar and all your people. Liars all.' She sat down. Ebo sat beside her, 'Please Bisi. Trust me, it will be all right. Don't worry, you and the boys

3

will be safe. Please . . .'

Ebo was worried after this incident. He was determined that he and his family would survive the war. He owed it as a duty to his wife, and his children. To better support his family, he gave forged passes, which he got as a D.M.I. Officer, to friends and relatives who paid him in cash and kind. He wondered whether Bisi knew how he got the money he gave her for house-keeping. She did not ask questions though, preoccupied as she was with the business of surviving.

Ebo's family had been in Okporo village for a month when his childhood friend, Eze, visited them with his wife, Adamma. Eze's home had been evacuated and the prospect of being refugees was irksome to Eze and his wife, because a refugee was more likely to be conscripted into the army. To Adamma's surprise, Ebo demanded ten Nigerian pounds in coins from his friend. Eze said nothing. It was his wife who spoke. 'Ebo,' she said quietly. 'Please have pity on us. We don't have one pound in Nigerian coins. Eze and I were married only a few months ago. We have lost everything. The vandals set our town on fire. Please say something we can afford. We can pay you in Biafran currency, that we can manage.'

There was an awkward silence, then Bisi emerged from the room and summoned her husband to follow her. Soon he came out again and demanded five Nigerian pounds in coins. Eze agreed to pay one. Then Bisi came out again and shouted at her husband, 'Ebo, enough of this. Eze, you pay nothing. Here you are,' and she handed Eze a uniform and identity card duly signed. 'Eze, you are Ebo's friend.

War or no war, we must remember our friends. So go into the room and put on the uniform,' she said.

Ebo stared at his wife in utter disbelief. Was Bisi mad? Eze and his wife stared as well, not knowing what to do next. Then Bisi sat down on the floor, crossed her legs and said, 'Let me tell you a dream. I dreamt last night I was in Lagos, or was it Ibadan. You see I am from Ijebu Ode but my parents live in Lagos. Anyway, in the dream I got married to Ebo in Lagos. It was a gorgeous white wedding. The Prime Minister attended, and twenty top army officers. My husband was a colonel in the army. All my brides-maids were flown from Paris and my flower girls were from Athens. And the wedding cake? That was made in Lisbon. There were three wedding cakes. But the plane did not arrive on time. No, it was not the plane. My husband was arrested on the day of the wedding. Ask me why? Simply because he refused to fly the plane. So the airport commandant arrested him, and arrested my three wedding cakes. And I stood at the altar waiting for the bridegroom who had flown to Lisbon to bring in arms that would be used to clear the vandals from the mysterious Lake.

'But people in Owerri were angry. They said, why should my husband fly to Lisbon to bring in arms and ammunition to clear the vandals from Lake Oguta, while Owerri was threatened? So they arrested my husband, and I stood at the altar waiting. Then the priest said, "You beautiful bride without a bridegroom, be my wife." Then I said to the priest, you good for nothing priest, you were the cause of this war. Your sins caused God's wrath, and God has descended on us. Why should I marry you? Do priests marry? Yes, priests do marry in Biafra. But I won't marry you because I am already married to Ebo. Ebo, my love, isn't that so?

'So the priest and . . .'

'Bisi, Bisi, stop it. I say stop it.' Ebo took hold of his wife and shook her vigorously. 'You are with me, we were married in Lagos all right. Come in, my love, come in and have a rest, you are tired. Oh, my God, Bisi, it will be perfectly all right. Take my word for it. We shall overcome. Biafra will win this war and I will take you back to Lagos and Ibadan and God and . . . '

'Don't get excited, my husband. Don't you ever get excited any more. I am not mad. I am quite sane. You are my husband. The man over there is your friend, Eze. You told me about him when you were courting me. And you wanted him to pay you five Nigerian pounds in coins. I ask you, will you eat money? You have a hundred pounds in coins. You gave it to me for safe keeping. What are you doing with your friend's coins? Tonight, you will go to the airport. The plane will bring in your worthless Biafran notes. You and your so-called friends will steal a carton each from the plane before lorries convey the money to the Central Bank.

'But, as I was saying, I told you I had a dream. There were people playing in a football pitch. Two teams. One was from Biafra and the other from Zambia, or was it Tanzania? Then ten MIGs from Egypt descended on the players and bombed them all out of the football field. Yes, it was at the Liberty Stadium, Ibadan. Not one spectator reached home. They were all killed by the MIGs flown by the wicked Egyptians.

'God works in a mysterious way. Not one of the players lost his life. Then a huge plane from China landed at Liberty Stadium and air-lifted all the players. The Nigerians were still in confusion. And do you know where the Chinese plane landed? Not at Uli airstrip — it was too small for the plane. Not at Uga airstrip either. It landed on Lake Oguta and the players all swam out to safety.

'So you see, I lost my father and my mother and my brothers and sisters. They were in the Liberty Stadium on that fateful day. So Ebo my husband had brought me here to die in the hands of the villagers. So help me beg Ebo to take me away from this village before I commit suicide. Help me tell Ebo to put me in the Red Cross plane tonight at all costs.

'He deceived me. He told me the war would be over in two weeks, that the Israelis were on our side. It was one of his friends who lied to the people of Biafra, telling them that all the countries in the world had recognised Biafra. Now he has brought me here to live and die like a rat. So that . . .'

Adamma, Eze's wife, got up now and whispered to Ebo's wife, who followed her out of the house, 'You are tired, you must sleep. This war is terrible, but please don't let it get you. I married only a few months ago, and I don't want it to get me. I must survive this war. Please don't let it get you. Where are your children?'

'With the priest. They are being baptised for the fourth time since the beginning of this war. I told the priest I did not want his relief. I never could eat stockfish. Egg yolk made me sick. All I wanted from him was milk and sugar and coffee and flour. Then he began to make certain demands, so I stopped

7

going and sent my boys instead.'

Inside the house, Ebo's head was bowed low. This was it. His wife was now mad. He must look for a psychiatrist to treat her. There was only one of note in the whole of Biafra and he had almost worked himself to death. Poor doctor. Why on earth did he take to that kind of specialisation? All sorts of patients were brought to him: those who suffered from shell-shock and other shocks, those who ran amok in broad daylight, and those wives whose husbands had died in battle fields and those declared missing. All flocked to the good doctor. Was Ebo's wife going to be one of them? No, she must be flown to Lisbon by any means. That night if possible.

Ebo woke up at midnight. He woke his wife and children. He asked his wife to dress and he dressed the children himself.

'Where are we going?' Bisi asked.

'We are going on a long journey. Please don't ask any more questions. Just do as I ask you,' he commanded. Then he called his driver and gave him a message to the commandant of the Uli Airstrip. 'Tell the commandant that a very important person and his family are leaving tonight for Lisbon. The Airstrip must be well guarded,' the message read.

In half an hour, the driver was back. The message had been delivered. Ebo and his family waited for an hour, then proceeded to the airstrip.

Meanwhile the news had gone round at the airport that Her Excellency was travelling that night. The Queen of England had received the petition sent to her by the National Women's Club, the Busy Bee Women's Club, and the Women's Active Service Club. Her Majesty the Queen, and the Queen's

8

mother, were distressed by the sufferings of the innocent Biafran children. So Her Majesty the Queen had graciously sent for Her Excellency to have a woman to woman discussion on the help Great Britain could give to the suffering and peace loving people of Biafra.

The security was quite tight on that night. All those who were not supposed to be there disappeared. Nobody was sure whether His Excellency was seeing her off or not. So the airport officials needed to be quite prepared and be on their best behaviour. The fact that no official letter was received from Government House made the whole trip more authentic than ever.

Ebo and his family arrived just at the time the relief plane was touching ground. Fatigue men were busy unloading the plane. The pilot came down for a rest before taking off again. Ebo went straight to him and spoke to him. The pilot nodded without understanding a word of what Ebo said. He spoke only French and Spanish.

.Then shots were heard. Nigerian planes were above and were firing at the relief plane. This was Ebo's chance. The pilot climbed into his plane. Ebo's wife and children followed. The airport commandant was there. He bowed and smiled stupidly as they climbed into the plane. None of the people standing by had set eyes on the First Lady before. Before the door of the plane was shut, Ebo climbed in and the plane took off.

At Umuahia, the following morning, women leaders got together for once to protest to the Foreign Secretary about their non-inclusion in the mission. An inexperienced foreign affairs officer, who had abandoned his post in India, and had returned through the Cameroons just before war was declared, was at a loss what to say to the women. 'We demand to see the Foreign Secretary,' the women shouted.

'He has gone to the toilet,' the officer said.

'Rubbish. You civil servants, when will you stop your lies? Haven't you any other excuse to make for your boss other than that? Toilet or no toilet we shall wait for him. It is inconceivable, honestly, I just cannot understand it.'

'You wait until we see him. He must explain. He must tell us who represents the women. You know, my driver came to me early this morning and gave me the news. He was so concerned. A fellow driver had told him that some women had been sent to London to represent the Biafran women. He knew that I represented all the women in Biafra, so he had come to tell me. He felt it was most unfair,' one of the women leaders reported, indignantly.

Unfortunately for the officer, the door opened and the Foreign Secretary appeared. 'We have come to see you. But we were told you went to the toilet. Tell us, if the Queen of England wanted to have an audience with the representatives of Biafran women, who should be asked to represent them?'

'Please sit down, ladies. I don't quite understand your question.'

'Are you aware, or are you not aware that some woman left Biafra only last night for Britain?'

'I am sorry, ladies, but kindly sit down. You see, there is so much to do and one gets strained and . . .'

'Please answer a simple question.' It was a young lawyer who spoke.

'I beg your pardon, ladies, but . . .' The telephone rang. He picked it up. 'Hello, yes, oh. Not now. My hands are full now. I have . . . Well in ten minutes . . . a cable, from where? . . not a cable . . . No. I am not aware. Intelligence Officer? With a foreign wife? . . . I'll be over shortly. Bye for now.' He replaced the telephone, and looked grave. Why did he not remain in the United States where he represented Nigeria at the United Nations? His job was not all that easy, but it was safe and secure. He had returned home to face Biafra and her women. The women. How could he cope with them? His wife could have helped him, but the women had successfully turned his wife against him, so that he was obliged to send her and his children to the village. Why could not the women organise themselves in one body and have just one leader? Why must every one of them want to lead? In this world there were leaders as well as followers. But here in Biafra each one of them must form her own group and dominate the other. He had to personally intervene in Enugu when two groups of women almost clashed openly. It needed all his diplomatic manoeuvres to calm them down. He did not see why women should not form groups and affiliate to whomsoever they wanted. He did not see why this could not be done peacefully. He did not see why they should compete with one another since they were all bent on one objective — to make Biafra a great nation.

The Foreign Secretary tried to crack a few jokes, but the moment had not come for jokes, only war reports! Yes, that could help, that is after he had calmed them down.

'I am sorry I cannot serve you coffee. We are at

11

war and . . .'

'Anybody who drinks coffee when the gallant Biafran forces are dying to save Biafra must be shot. So let's face our problem,' the young lawyer said.

'I drank coffee last in Enugu, and I don't even miss it. Coffee is the product of the imperialists who have bluntly refused to support Biafra. We shall deal with them when we win this war. None of them will be allowed in our land,' another said.

'I have some kolanuts here. My wife sent them to me from the village, please eat them before we start our discussion.' He was gradually winning over the women. He broke the kolanuts and they ate. Then the leader of the National Women's Club began, but she was soon interrupted by the young lawyer who told her that she had no right to speak first. Her organisation had its origins in Europe and America but Europe and America had bluntly refused to recognise Biafra. The lawyer's own organisation was the genuine one, free from the shackles of imperialism. It was high time Europe and America copied Africa. Biafra should show a good example. We had rejected everything Nigerian, and yet we still clung to an organisation in which Nigeria was a member.

The National Women's Club leader ignored her completely and continued, 'We are the accredited representatives of three women's organisations: the Busy Bee Club (B.B.C.), the Women's Active Service (W.A.S.) and the National Women's Club (N.W.C.). We have been told that Her Majesty the Queen of England wanted an audience with the representatives of Biafran women. And that the Biafran government sent an unknown group of women to Her Majesty the Queen.'

'When was this?' the Foreign Secretary asked.

'Last night. Only last night. We received the information from a good source. So don't you be clever with us. Who were the women you sent to Britain?'

'Who is your source?'

'We are not here to be asked questions,' the leader of the B.B.C. snapped. 'Did you or did you not send a group of women to Britain last night?'

'We did not, madam.'

'None of your madam here, Sir. We are ladies and must be addressed as such. You wait until the end of this war. There is going to be another war, the war of the women. You have fooled us enough. You have used us enough. You have exploited us enough. When this war has ended we will show you that we are a force to be reckoned with. You wait and see. What do you think we are? Instruments to be used and discarded?'

'My lady lawyer, if I must be crucified, at least I must be told my offence,' the Foreign Secretary said. He was now relaxed. He could now deal with the problem. There was absolutely nothing to hide. No such directive came from Her Majesty the Queen. So why worry?

'Your offence is that you by-passed us. Without the women, the Nigerian vandals would have overrun Biafra; without the women, our gallant Biafran soldiers would have died of hunger in the war fronts. Without the women, the Biafran Red Cross would have collapsed. It was my organisation that organised the kitchens and transport for the Biafran forces. You men went to the office every day doing nothing, busy but doing nothing.'

When the B.B.C. leader finished, the young lawyer took over. As for the N.W.C. leader, she was calm and collected. 'We are the indigenous group. We have been poised for action ever since war was declared. We are independent. We are not affiliated to any redundant and planless group. We are the creation of Biafra and our aim is to win the war for Biafra. Right from the word go, we organised the women for a real fight. We asked for guns to fight the enemy. We asked to be taught how to shoot. Did not women and girls fight in Vietnam? We asked to be taught how to take cover and how to evacuate women and children. But those who did not understand mounted strong propaganda against us. They said we were upsetting the women. But we were realistic. We knew Nigeria would fight us, so we must be prepared. Now after all we did in Enugu and are still doing in Umuahia, you had the impudence to send an unknown handful of women to represent Biafran women. It is most unfair. I have never seen anything like this before, it is . . .'

'Wait and hear from the Foreign Secretary,' the N.W.C's leader said. She was more experienced than the other two. She had been watching the Foreign Secretary, and suspected that they might not be correct after all. If the Foreign Secretary was trying to hide something, she would have known.

'Ladies, you know me very well. I was with you at Enugu. I helped you draft a petition to Her Majesty the Queen and to all prominent women of the world. I advised you that the petitions must not be cyclostyled, but typed separately. I gave you the correct titles and the addresses when you had trouble with the presentation of used clothes to the army. I stepped in and straightened everything. You are all women. I have a wife who is a woman. I have sisters and I have a mother. I swear by my mother that the Biafran government received no such request from Her Majesty the Queen or from any other prominent woman in the world. What you heard is absolutely untrue.'

'This is terrible,' the militant lawyer said. She had cross-examined criminals so she knew the Foreign Secretary was telling the truth.

'I'd advise you to go home and continue the good work. Soon we are going to have women guests from abroad.'

'But who were the women the driver said he saw boarding the plane last night? I have no reason to disbelieve him. He was always sure of his facts, Sir,' the N.W.C.'s leader continued. 'You must investigate this matter. There must be something going on. I don't know, but my feminine intuition tells me that the story is not altogether untrue. Mind you, I am not doubting you. But, you know what I mean.'

Of course the Foreign Secretary knew what she meant. Feminine intuition. That was what his wife used to win every argument. He must investigate of course. Somebody was up to something. He thanked the women and they left. He got up, lit his cigarette and began to smoke. Then he dialled a number, spoke and walked out of the office. There was a sharp pain in his stomach; it was his ulcer. When the war ended, he would have an operation.

DADDY, DON'T STRIKE
THE MATCH

Ifeoma rushed up to her father's bedroom screaming. Her father got up and carried her. 'What is the matter?' he said. 'One of her dreams again, Ifeoma's mother said, before her daughter had time to reply.

The child was shaking with sobs. 'They were running after me. They had guns and matchets. They painted their bodies with white chalk. One wanted to shoot me. He aimed his gun at me. Then Francis came in and pointed his toy gun at the soldier. "I will shoot you," Francis said. Then a big cow came and chased us, and chased us. Daddy, it was a very big cow. It was bigger than this house. I saw it. It was white and had black spots. Then I ran to you. Daddy, I am afraid. Daddy, when will they stop this war? I want to go back to Kano, daddy. I want to go back to school again daddy. I am missing my friend Jumai, and others. Oh daddy, can't we go back to Kano tomorrow? Please . . .'

'It's all right, my doll. It is perfectly all right. Nothing will happen to us. You were dreaming. There were no soldiers running after you. There was no cow either. It will be all right. Drink something and go to bed.'

'But daddy, there were soldiers with guns. I saw them with my own eyes. They wanted to shoot me. Then the cow came. I saw them, daddy. Mummy, didn't you see them?'

'I saw them, my love. Go to bed. Nothing will happen to you. Daddy is here, I am here. See, all the doors are locked. No harm will come to you, my

16

love.' Ifeoma's mother carried her to the kitchen to get her something to drink.

There were four tins of Ovaltine, large ones. Ifeoma's mother had a week before exchanged a carved ebony head for four tins of Ovaltine. In Kano her four children all drank Ovaltine before they went to bed. The children missed it in Biafra. The good white Rev. Father Anthony had asked her that morning whether she had anything for the pilots, not mercenary pilots, but pilots who risked their lives flying in relief materials to blockaded Biafra. Those good people, the Rev. Father said, were ordinary people with wives and children. When they went home, their wives and children would like to see something from the much talked about Biafra.

Ndidi Okeke had nothing of value but the ebony head which her husband bought years ago. She had been careful to bring back nearly all their property from Kano. A good friend, an expatriate, had told her in the school where she was teaching, 'Something dreadful will happen to your people sooner or later. I'd advise you to leave. Your husband, I know, is stubborn and talks too much, like your people. Persuade him to leave with you. If he refuses to leave, leave with your children. When the time comes, nobody will ask him to leave. He is a man, he will have no difficulty at all.'

The friend refused to discuss the matter any further, nor would she answer any of Ndidi's numerous questions, nor talk to her again about this impending doom of her people. Ndidi told her husband, who dismissed it as gossip. Everything was perfectly all right: there was peace, there was stability.

But Ndidi saw one or two of her people in Kano and began to make preparations. She hired two lorries at a fantastic price, triple the normal charge, and packed everything, including her brooms, into the lorries. They were going to Enugu. That was the destination of everybody in 1966 and 1967. Mr. Okeke refused to leave; his wife had failed to convince him of the imminent danger.

She hired a flat, again the rent was triple what was the normal rent, but she did not mind. She had transferred nearly two thousand pounds to the bank at Enugu. This was her own money, not her husband's. She was teaching and also doing some contract work in Kano. She spent very little on food for they owned a farm. She did not buy rice or yams, she got these from the contract work she did. She lacked nothing. And her husband did not control her finances. Whatever she earned she spent on herself and her children. What a pity that she was leaving Kano. Kano, where she was born, where her placenta was buried. Where her parents lived for thirty years, and left because they were getting too old and wanted to go home and die quietly.

Now, in the outlandish place near Orlu where her husband worked with the Research and Production group (R.A.P.), she had nothing of value but an ebony head. Ndidi and her husband were away for the weekend when Enugu was about to fall. Her husband, like the man he was, had raced back to Enugu from Awka to see what he could evacuate. A part of Enugu was being shelled when he entered Uwani from Agbani. He got his children's clothes, his wife's, a suit and a few shirts and that ebony head, and drove back. He was brave. If he had dilly-dallied, he would have been captured. One of his friends who risked the journey with him did not return.

Ndidi Okeke gave the ebony head to Rev. Father Anthony. And he gave her in exchange four tins of Ovaltine for her children.

Ifeoma was still crying when she came into the kitchen. Her mother set her down on a stool while she made the Ovaltine for her. The three boys were sleeping soundly. The oldest was fifteen and very tall, and he was restricted at home. If he wandered about in the village, he might be conscripted into the army. At this time, Mr. Okeke came into the kitchen and sat down waiting for Ifeoma to drink her Ovaltine and go back to bed. 'Daddy, when will the war end?' Ifeoma asked her father and came over to him and sat on his lap. 'I am afraid, daddy. I am afraid of cows, of soldiers and of air-raids, Daddy, why are they bombing us? Why are the vandals so wicked, daddy? I want to go back to Kano. I want the war to end so that I can go back to school. I like school, daddy. I like our white Rev. Sister. Will I see her again, daddy? And daddy . . .'

She went on in this way. The Ovaltine was made, she drank it and wanted more. Ndidi made another one. She drank half of it and dozed off on her father's lap. Ndidi covered up the remaining Ovaltine. She did not drink it, it was the children's. She had determined to sell the five pieces of 'abada' she had to feed her children. She dreaded kwashiokor. She would rather die than see her children suffer from the dreaded disease of the civil war, which was feared more than leprosy.

Mr. Okeke put his daughter to bed. He went back

to bed. His wife was wide awake. He struck a match and looked at the watch on the crude table. It was three in the morning. Before he put out the match, he was able to see the face of his wife. Fear was written on her lovely face. Fear of the war, fear of what might happen to them when and not if, Biafra was over-run. For Ndidi Okeke was sure Biafra would be over-run eventually. She had told her husband so many times. He had quarrelled with her each time she said it, but since Aba fell soon after Port Harcourt, he had talked less and became less optimistic. But he had gone on working with normal zeal. He was a dedicated and honest Biafran. He saw what happened in Kano. He escaped death by a narrow margin. He watched where he was in hiding, his friends shot in cold blood. He was too involved in the war right from the beginning. He had contributed a lot to the defence of Biafra. He would continue to give his knowledge and time and, if need be, his life to Biafra.

His wife was not so inclined. All she wished for was that the war should come to an end so that they would go back to Kano. It was a simple childlike wish, like her daughter's. What else could a normal mother of four children wish for in a time like that?

'The children, we can take care of ourselves. Four children, including Martin. Every day I live in fear. Fear that Martin will one day be conscripted. Fear that one day one of us or all of us will die in an air-raid,' Ndidi said.

'I share all your fears,' her husband said.

'But we have to live like everybody else. It is our fate.'

'We cannot escape, you know it. And . . .'

'We can. I have told you we can.'
'Not with four children, Martin, especially. See how tall he is. We can't, Ndidi, you know we can't. I am in R.A.P. you know. I am not one of the top ones, but, well you know what I mean. Everything has an end. The Nigeria—Biafra war will one day come to an end. Try and sleep. You have lost so much weight of late. Don't worry yourself too much. Millions of us are involved in this war. It is not just Okeke's family, but millions of families.'
'I am frightened of air-raids. Look, parents can no longer protect their children. When our children are afraid, we are afraid as well. We all hide in the bunker trembling with fear. And have you noticed Ifeoma of late? At first she used to cry when there was an air-raid. Now she does not cry. She laughs instead. She laughs continuously until after the air-raid. Of course, what am I saying, you are always in the lab when there is an air-raid. Poor girl. When I see her laughing, I feel my heart breaking. It's all a dream. One day it will end. All will end, and we will go back to Kano. I was born and bred there. I know nothing of our people. They accused me of behaving like Kano people. I came home only three times before I married you. I speak the language all right, but it is to me a second language. Hausa is my language. It was my first language. So, I do not.'
'It's all right. Don't talk any more.' He held her and kissed her. 'It will end. Take life as you see it. We shall survive. The suffering will end. I have succeeded in getting Martin a pass. He always has his birth certificate with him. So have no fear, he will not be conscripted.'
'So Dan's father said to his wife. Then one day

21

Dan went to collect relief from the mission and did not return. We later heard that he was conscripted. By the time his father found petrol to go to Nnewi where Dan was taken to, he had gone to the Onitsha war front. And nothing has been heard about him since then. He is only sixteen. But our Martin is taller. We are not sure of anything now. All you have to do is to get an officer's uniform for Martin. He is tired of hiding. One day he will be so bored that he will walk out on us . . .'

'Petrol won't be our problem. We make petrol, Ndidi, that's my job. To make petrol and other things.'

'You are joking again. You joke about everything these days, even your life you joke about.'

Mr. Okeke was at a loss what else to say. Women, they were all the same. So unreasonable, so adamant. What did his wife want him to do then? To escape? Where was their desination going to be, Enugu? The scientists in R.A.P. were all known by the Nigerian intelligence service by name. They would kill him if they caught him. No, there was nothing to be done. All they had to do was to keep alive in Biafra.

'No, my wife, I am not joking. There is nothing to be done.' He got up, made for the table and got hold of a Mars cigarette packet. He struck the match, and his wife jumped up from the bed. 'What is it?' she said in fright.

'Ndidi, it is only a match. I wanted to smoke. Is that what frightened you so much? Your nerves are all shattered. You were not like this last night. What has come over you this morning? You have been brave. Do you remember when you were demonstrating with the women in Enugu? You were

22

carrying a placard "Ojukwu give us guns". You were in the forefront. What has happened to your courage?'

'You are joking again. There is no end to what you can joke about. However, before you distract me from what I wanted to say, it is about time you stopped smoking. Why, you didn't smoke before the war. Why then are you smoking now, when cigarettes are so expensive and hard to come by? You smoke nearly two packets of Mars a day. Can't you curtail it? Can't you stop it entirely? I don't like the smell of Mars.'

'Well, I can smoke Benson and Hedges then if you don't like the smell of Mars.'

'Stop smoking. That's what I am telling you.'

'I will not stop smoking, Ndidi. Enough of this. Now, go to bed.'

Mrs. Okeke apologised. She had gone too far, and she knew it. She was a good wife and she knew when to stop. She wrapped herself up in her blanket, and faced the wall. After a long time, she fell asleep.

Mr. Okeke finished his cigarette. He went to the kitchen, drank the Ovaltine that was left, a little water, and went to sleep. He slept immediately his head touched the pillow.

Ndidi heard a faint knock. She knew it was her little daughter, Ifeoma. She got up and opened the door quietly for her.

'Now, don't wake daddy up,' she said quietly. 'Come and lie down here.'

'I don't want to lie down. I am hungry. And I have had my bath.' Ifeoma said. It was then that Ndidi looked at her husband's watch and knew that it was seven thirty.

'Mummy, I am hungry,' Ifeoma said again. 'I want my Ovaltine.' Ndidi did not want to mention the incident of the night. But as soon as she heard the word Ovaltine, her heart missed a beat. She was afraid that Ifeoma would remember what she suffered in the night.

'I want to drink the Ovaltine I do not finish yesterday.' Ifeoma said.

'I did not finish' Mrs. Okeke corrected.

'I did not finish' Ifeoma replied. Ndidi was particular about grammar. War or no war, her children must speak correctly. She was after all a teacher. A Maths teacher. She did Maths at Ibadan. English was her subsidiary subject. She was relaxing now because of the stresses of war. Her protected children were now mixing with children of the village. Raw parents who did not teach their raw children hygiene. Why should this happen to her? Her children who were used to using toilets now went to the bush to do the thing. There was no toilet paper. The last one she bought, that was at Owerri, cost her nearly ten shillings. This was soon after the fall of Port Harcourt. The Biafran pound had not lost its value then. A kind Rev. Sister had given her some toilet rolls at one time, but she had asked for Quaker Oats instead.

'Is Keziah up,' she asked her daughter.

'Keziah went to the stream,' she replied. By this time, Mr. Okeke was up.

'You and your daughter won't let me sleep. Now come along Ifeoma and sleep beside me; while mummy makes you a fresh Ovaltine.'

'I want the one from last night,' Ifeoma said.

'Oh, that one. I drank it. Daddy was hungry so he

drank it.'

'Ehee, daddy was hungry, the child chorused, doubtful that daddies, least of all her own daddy could be hungry.

'Daddy,' Ifeoma said.

'Yes, my angel,' There was pain in his eyes now, because he knew what was coming next.

'The white cow with black spots; has it gone?'

'Yes, my love. It has gone.'

'Did you drive it away last night?'

'Yes, my love, I drove it away,' he said.

'It did not hurt you, daddy?'

'No, it did not hurt me.'

'And the soldiers. Did they shoot you?'

'No, they did not shoot me. I drove them away. They will not come again.'

'They will not come again?' she asked doubtfully.

'No, they are all dead.'

'Did you shoot them, daddy?'

Mr. Okeke realised too late that he should not have said that. Death was all around. Why mention it, especially to a frightened and nervous child?

'Ik said he shot two soldiers.'

'When?' Mr. Okeke asked, feigning interest.

'Yesterday when they went for combing.'

'Combing? Did Ik go to comb yesterday?'

'Yes, he went. Ik told me. He said Martin took him to comb the bushes yesterday.'

'Go and call me Ik and Martin,' Mr. Okeke said. He was frightened.

Martin and Ik came in and Mr. Okeke fired questions at his children.

'Did you go to comb yesterday?'

'No, daddy,' Martin replied.

'Ifeoma said you went to comb. That you took Ik with you.'

Both boys began to laugh. Ifeoma was full of imaginings these days.

'She must have dreamt it,' Ik volunteered to explain.

'Ifeoma dreams a lot these days, daddy. The other night, she told me she dreamt that she was flying an enemy's plane. And that they bombed a school and a hospital.'

'Did she say it? Ifeoma, come my brave girl, did you dream that you were a pilot, sent on a mission to bomb?'

'Yes,' Ifeoma smiled mischievously. 'But I won't go again daddy.' Ifeoma said.

'No, don't go again. It is too dangerous.'

'Yes, and I don't like it, daddy. I don't like killing people,' Ifeoma said.

'It is bad. We should not kill.'

Ndidi came in at last with four cups of Ovaltine. It took so much time to make these days. There were no tins of milk but powdered milk. You had to beat and beat before the lumps dissolved properly. Her entrance was a great relief, for Mr. Okeke was getting more and more involved with his children's questions.

All the children were in the room now. They drank their Ovaltine. Mr. Okeke went to have his bath at the back of the house. When he came back, the children were still there. 'Now you go to your room while I get dressed. I am late for work.'

'Daddy,' Martin began.

'Yes.' Mr. Okeke turned to his eldest son.

'Daddy, you make bombs in the lab?'

26

'Yes we do.'

'Will you teach me how to make bombs?'

'No' Mr. Okeke said bluntly.

'Why, daddy?'

'They are very dangerous to make. And you remember, you told me you were going to be a doctor. You will learn to save people's lives, and not to destroy them.'

'Bombs destroy life?' Ifeoma asked.

'Yes, don't you know?' Ik asked.

'And daddy, you make them,' Ifeoma accused.

Mr. Okeke felt a sharp pain somewhere inside him. He had felt that pain before. When was it? He remembered but did not want to recall it. It was very painful.

And here was Ifeoma, his own daughter accusing him. And he felt the sharp pain again. The pain he felt looking at the accusing face of the dying youth, barely two months ago.

'Take your children away so I can dress up for work,' he called to Ndidi, who took the children away amidst protests from Ifeoma and the youngest boy.

When Mr. Okeke finished dressing, he had his breakfast. All the time his mind was on the accusation of Ifeoma and the experiments he was setting up in the lab.

It was usual for him to smoke a cigarette after breakfast. The box of matches was not there. So he went to the room, got it and lit a cigarette. Then he remembered what his wife said. He did not see why he should be a chain-smoker now. He had smoked when he was at college. Before he graduated, he had given it up. And he did not smoke ever again, until

27

the war. The stresses and strains of the war probably made him start smoking again.

He got ready. He called his wife. 'I am going.' he shouted. The children came round.

'I'll come with you,' Ifeoma said.

'No please, children don't go there.'

'I'll come then,' Martin said. 'I am a big boy of fifteen.'

'Yes, you are a big boy, but not so big.' Oh, not again, Mr. Okeke said under his breath. 'These children,' he said under his breath again.

He went at last. About an hour later, somebody came from the lab for Mr. Okeke's cigarettes and a box of matches. He had forgotten them when he was going to work.

It was Ndidi who had found them. 'Perhaps John is going to stop smoking at last,' she mused and put them away. 'You have come for master's cigarettes and box of matches,' Ndidi asked.

'Yes,' the lab attendant said. Ndidi asked Keziah to go for them. Then Ifeoma came in. 'Mummy can I take them to him?'

'No love, here is the lab attendant. He has come for them.'

'Take me with you, attendant,' Ifeoma pleaded.

The boy smiled and said nothing. Ifeoma watched the lab attendant leaving with the cigarettes and the matches, Then she shouted, 'Attendant!'. The boy turned round. Ifeoma said, 'Tell daddy not to strike the match.'

The boy smiled and went away, immediately forgetting the child's joke. Ifeoma went on playing. After some time, she said, 'Daddy don't strike the match.' Then she began to sing it. Her mother was busy in the kitchen. She did not hear her. The children did not take any notice of her.

Mr. Okeke's group had a short meeting. And everybody went to his own assignment. He had been setting up the experiment for some time, and he was succeeding, but he never discussed his job at home. Ndidi was a Maths teacher all right, but she was not interested in the experiments. As a matter of fact, all she was interested in was the survival of her children, herself and her husband, and her dear ones. Experiment or no experiment, Biafra was not going to win. She had said this to her husband. And he refused to speak to her for nearly a week.

He had worked for several hours, with nothing to eat, but he was not hungry. There had been a difficult problem to which he had not found a solution. Now it seemed as if he was going to find a solution at last after the short meeting with his fellow scientists.

It was not till five o'clock that he felt satisfied with what he was doing. He threw his head back. At long last it was set. The job had been done. Then the urge came to smoke. The packet of cigarettes was some distance away, while the box of matches was in his pocket. Yes, he had left them in his pocket so that nobody would use them. It was dangerous.

He observed something near the experiment which baffled him and looked over it again. 'Why?' he asked himself. Then he saw it, and put it right in a few minutes.

He deserved a cigarette. He struck the match. Before he realised what had happened, he was in the midst of a formidable fire. Everything was ablaze. It was terrible. Nobody heard his shouting. Nobody was in sight until a few minutes later when smoke was discovered coming from the room by passers by. They shouted.

Men rushed in. They were blinded by smoke. Where was a fire extinguisher? Was there none? No water, no sand, no nothing? Mr. Okeke? It was then that it dawned on Mr. Okeke's colleagues that he was in the lab.

Nobody could get in. The lab was highly inflammable. It consumed Okeke and his experiment.

A CERTAIN DEATH

He was about eighteen years old, fair, very handsome and well built. I kept staring at him when he stood at attention and saluted me in military style. My mind was at rest. It was true what they had said of him.

The man had come to see us the previous day. I did not know him. I did not even know who had suggested to a friend that we should see him and that he would be able to help us.

This man was tough. It was not easy to place him. He was not an army officer. He did not look like a political thug nor a militia in the then Biafra. He was plain tough.

He spoke to my brother who was unwell. I was there beside him. Only a month ago, he had lost his wife and two children in a gruesome air-raid that struck in the market place. The wife was returning from the market, when the jets descended. She had no time to take cover. It appeared as if they had come purposely for her. In an instant, she was struck, and her head was severed from her body. Then the rest of the body convulsed in death throes, jerked a few yards, and died, a second time.

At that very moment, the two children playing in front of the house were killed in the same raid.

The people marvelled. 'The couple must be evil. Air raid, like thunder, doesn't strike innocent people. They must be guilty of some crime. A mother and her two children to die in one air raid! It is most unnatural.'

My brother went off his head. He was still dazed

as the remnants of flesh that were once his wife's and children's were gathered and put in one hurriedly made coffin.

'Throw them away, why bother to make a coffin,' some people had whispered. But I insisted that at least a coffin should be provided for the pieces of human flesh.

My mind went back to the first air raid in Port Harcourt. A prominent businessman had been struck as he was descending the steps of his storey building. The contents of his brief case had been revealed in which there was some deal with the Federal Military Government. And besides he was an evil and heartless businessman who did not hesitate to fight his business competitors with any available weapon. It was right and just that he should meet his death in the way he did.

I had believed everthing I heard about the man. And perhaps, if I were in Port Harcourt, I would have joined the crowd that went to see the pieces of flesh of a saboteur.

For days my brother was dazed. He could say nothing and he could eat nothing. I was beside him. I was then the only possession he had. I was his only sister. We had no brother. Our parents had died when we were young.

'Leave my brother alone,' I said to the man. 'I sent for you. Tell me what you want, and I'll give it to you. You see him there, he has nobody but me. I have nothing, but him. I'll sell myself to see that he does not go to war. So what do you want?'

'Young woman, please don't be so snappy. I want to help you. I have helped many like you. I am not a mercenary. You have a genuine case. They can shoot me if they know what I am trying to do. The youth I am going to bring to you tomorrow has been employed before by many people. This is not the first time nor the second. His father knows all about it. In fact the money we ask for would be sent to his father. His father is in great hardship. His children are starving. This is all the youth can do to help him and his young sisters and brothers.'

'You are most kind. I understand. Please pardon me. How much then?'

'Only four hundred pounds, and one hundred for me, and fifty for the youth to bribe his way through.'

I counted the money and gave it to him. He counted it very carefully. 'Keep fifty pounds,' he said. 'When I bring him in the morning, you give it to him. Four hundred pounds I'll give his father before he releases him to me.'

I was not engaged in the attack trade. I bought and sold in the local market while I waited for the war to end. I had sold two eight pieces of 'jorge' for five hundred pounds for this purpose. I did not want to borrow. Nobody would of course lend me money without asking questions.

What did I not do to save my brother from this certain death? Conscription was certain death for him. The people had demanded that he should go to war before he brought ruin to the town. Someone who lost a wife and two children in one day must be evil. He must have done something to merit the punishment. If he was not got rid of, the whole town would suffer.

I was trading in Lagos when the crisis started. I was the first among the other women trading in Balogun Street to return. My husband was working in one of the Ministries in Lagos. He was attending a course in the U.S.A. when the coup took place. He sent a frantic cable to me asking me to take our three children home immediately. I obeyed.

I hired a vehicle from a relation of my husband's, put my three children in the vehicle, and begged him to take them home, while I collected debts from my numerous debtors.

My children, the driver and my personal belongings never reached my home. There was an accident near Ore and all the passengers were killed. My husband preferred to remain in the U.S.A. after this tragedy.

Was there any wonder that our people were afraid that my brother and I could bring them further disaster? If they got rid of my brother by sending him to this certain death, they would avert the disaster. So I was bent on seeing that he was not sacrificed, even if it meant my own death.

So that morning, the youth was in front of me. 'Please sit down,' I said. He refused to sit down. The tough man had left. I could not help noticing that he left in a hurry and that there was pain in his eyes.

My brother came out this time and sat down in the only available chair. He was still unwell, and there was evidence that he had cried in the night. 'Did you hear them this morning?' he asked me. I nodded.

'Never mind,' I said. 'Nothing will happen to you. As long as I am alive nothing will ever happen to you.'

I hadn't told him what I intended doing. He saw the youth, but he had not the slightest idea of what he was doing in the house. I'll tell him, not now, later. If I told him then, he would ask questions and I was not prepared to give answers to the questions. I was bent on saving his life. Was I bent on killing the youth?

My blood ran cold. Kill the youth. Of course he was not going to die. I was assured. He had done it twice. The third time might be tough, might even cost him his life. God forbid! He will come back. He will surely come back. My God, what was happening to me? to us? to the whole world?

I got up. I called the maid. 'Agnes, please give him food to eat. I have everything prepared. I'll soon be back.'

What if he escaped when I was away? I had spent five hundred pounds already. I had nothing else left to sell except my bed. Perhaps I'd sell that too if he escaped. No, he will not escape. The tough man had reassured me. My brother did not ask me where I was going.

I knocked at the door of the man in charge of conscription. The door was opened and I walked in. He offered me a seat. I sat down and looked intently at him. He pretended not to know why I had come. The silence was getting longer, so he began: 'Just tell me why your brother should not fight for the liberation of Biafra?'

Instantly, I wanted to reply: 'And you, could you tell me why you yourself are in charge of conscription and not my brother?'

I restrained myself. There was absolutely no reason why I should be offensive. We were at war with the whole world. We were in a state of emergency. Unimportant people had overnight become Very Important People. If one played one's card very well, one would survive. I was not going to cause the death of my brother by being stupid. I had to be diplomatic.

'He is my only brother. He is all I have in the world. He has never killed a fly. Please help me. Do all you can for me. God will reward you. Everyone knows my story. Save my brother; you never know, this war will end, my brother may be of help to you in normal times. You know about my husband. They say he is dead, I don't think so. He is in America. He is quite high in government. You never can tell, he might be of use too. Please have pity.'

He smiled. 'My two children are in the army. We are at war with Nigeria. They killed us like flies in the north. We must fight for our freedom. There is no going back. It has come to the stage when all of us should be called. He must go. When I am called I too must go. Those Biafran youths dying were born of women. They were human beings like you and I. So I don't see why your brother should not go to war.'

He got up and said he was attending a meeting, and that he was in fact late already. I too got up. I was thinking fast. What was I going to do next? 'Where do I go?' I asked him.

'Go home,' he said irritably. I smiled.

'I am going home.'

He smiled in spite of himself. Then he said, not really to me but to himself, 'Ike Ugo must be asked to explain certain things about this conscription. He seems to be lukewarm about a number of things. However . . .'

'Who is Ike Ugo?' I asked myself as I went home with a heavy heart. 'I have heard of him. In what connection? In what connection? In what . . .'

Of course I knew Ike Ugo. In the good old days his sister and I were great friends. We both married, got busy in our homes and saw little of each other. I was not sure whether Ike would remember me. If his sister had returned as I did, it would have been easy, but she did not return. I must go to him, perhaps he had something to do with this conscription, otherwise the man in charge of conscription would not have mentioned his name. I could see that he was not pleased with the way Ike Ugo was handling things. Perhaps Ike was more humane about it all.

Ike was in. Fortunately, he remembered me. I asked about his sister and family. They were in Lagos, he said. Somehow, he went on, he managed to hear from them. He had heard about me and my woes, and he was very sorry. Then he said, 'What can I do for you, my sister's friend?'

Before I said anything, I wiped the tears from my eyes, then carefully, I told him the plight that I was in.

'You should not have gone to him,' he said. 'I am in charge of it all. Have you someone to go in place of your brother?'

'Yes,' I said.

'Can you bring him tomorrow to me in the office?'

'He is in my house right now' I said.

'You have no problem. I shall come and collect him when we finish the meeting. There is no problem at all. The youth would not even answer your brother's name. He would answer his own name. I shall tick your brother's name as having fulfilled all the conditions. Never mind. There is no problem.' At this juncture he enumerated the names of the people who had already passed through this ordeal. And added. 'Ask your brother to be scarce for at least three weeks.'

It was too good to be true. I got up. 'Ike,' I said. 'How do I thank you?' He only smiled.

'Don't worry. We shall all survive.'

I went home. The youth was there. He stood at attention again and saluted. Why is he so respectful? I wanted to ask him to confirm what I had heard of him, namely, that it was his will and that of his father that he should employ himself in this way. That he knew his way about and had in fact gone to fight in place of two people in the past. But I had no courage to ask him. He was too handsome, too young to employ himself in that dangerous way. And besides I wanted at all costs to save the life of my only brother.

I asked Agnes whether he had eaten. 'Yes, he has eaten,' she said and smiled. 'He ate up everything and asked, shyly, for more.'

'And did you give him?'

'No, I didn't. That was all I had for him.'

I wanted to call Agnes all sorts of names I could think of, but restrained myself. I went to the kitchen and prepared something quickly for the youth. He was grateful. He ate up everything again.

At this time, my brother was out and I waited for Ike to come. I prayed that he should come before my brother returned from wherever he went. I wanted to spare him the agony of any further transaction that might ensue again. He knew I was up to something. But he did not want to discuss it. He was really not interested in anything.

'I lost my wife and children the same day. What else matters? If they want me to go to war, I'll go. It is the easiest way to die these days. Nobody would accuse you of suicide.'

Suicide it was. To be compelled to go to war and

to be conscripted into the Biafran army was suicide, pure and simple. Only those who possessed the 'sixth sense' survived. Like the youth who was now going to take the place of my brother. I had bought him to 'die' in place, not of, but for my brother. Nobody was prepared to die for anybody. But why should anyone want to die for another? It did not make sense at all. Death was no joke. If you died, you died, and that was the end of you.

'We shall all survive.' The words of Ike kept ringing in my ears. Perhaps we shall all survive. Who knows? Perhaps we should all die before the war ended. Who knows? Only God knew. God, please be merciful to us and save us from death, from air raids, from accidental discharges, from night-marauders, from deserters, from saboteurs, from white mercenaries, from overzealous leaders.

I waited for Ike for nearly an hour, but he did not come. An unknown fear gripped me. Why hadn't he come? He said he would come and take the youth immediately. No, he said he would attend a meeting first. Which meeting was that? There were so many meetings in those days. People simply loved meetings. One did not only go to a meeting to air one's views; one went to listen and to be listened to. One wanted to score points. To bring it to the knowledge of everyone that one knew how to talk, that one was very important.

The youth was there. He was so relaxed and this comforted me. It made me relax as well for a little while. I waited for Ike. He will come. He was such a nice person. He was not going to let me down.

Then I heard a conversation. It was coming nearer and nearer. 'What he was saying,' said one, 'was that nobody was too big to go to war. That he had sacrificed two of his sons and so everybody should sacrifice his sons as well.'

'No, that was not what he meant exactly. What he meant was that he had already sacrificed two boys in the war, and everybody should do the same. Everybody who had sons to sacrifice. I have no male child, thank God.'

'Childless mothers seem to be quite happy at this conscription you know.'

'Why not? Conscription is certain death. The quickest way to die. Those conscripted have no training at all. Didn't you know?'

Did the youth hear? Perhaps he heard. Was he still willing to go? What if he melted away before Ike came? I had paid for him to replace my brother. If he disappeared without fulfilling the contract there was nothing I could do. Nothing. Absolutely nothing. God have mercy on us.

At last Ike came. He was in a hurry. 'Where is he?' he asked.

I took him to where the boy was. 'Let's go then, they are waiting for us.'

The youth got up, and obeyed. I pressed fifty pounds into his palm. He gripped the money. He did not turn back. I watched him go with Ike. Why should people go to war? Why should people resort to force? I was sending this boy, who was old enough to be my son to a certain death. No, I was not. He was not going to fight. He said he had gone twice. This was his third time. He said he was well known in Orlu and therefore would not want to go there. He was going to Owerri. He was not known in Owerri. He knew his way about. I should not worry.

But I worried as Ike took him. I had seen those conscripted before. They looked wretched. There was one particular one who wept all through. He did not return. His aged mother is still waiting for him. He will never return.

About a week later, early in the morning, the crier piped out: 'The village of Amosu, the village of Amosu. Do you hear? Open your ears and hear me. You are in arrears of men for the army. Do you hear, you are in arrears of men. This is the last warning. On Afo day, you must present the men for the army. If you don't your village head will be handed over to the army. Don't say you were not warned. You are the only village in arrears.'

I shivered. The youth had replaced my brother, thank God. My brother had left the town. Nobody would see him until this cruel war was over.

41

MAN PALAVER

Adaku was the mother of seven children who lived with her family in Lagos. Her husband was a simple and hard-working man who worked in one of the Ministries. Since appointed, he had refused to take any bribe from anybody, no matter the temptation. Adaku was envious of her husband's colleagues, who made it to the top fast, because they knew how to play the game. She nagged her husband, but he told her in his quiet way that he could never sleep peacefully once he took bribes, it was not in his nature to be corrupt and that she should please, for the sake of the children, leave him alone.

Adaku was not by nature greedy but the strain of taking care of seven children and working full-time was telling on her. She had to make do with the meagre food money her husband gave her every month. She went to markets she thought were cheap and bought foodstuffs. She economised, but everything was becoming too expensive. She was just thinking that she should look for a good psychiatrist to confide in, when her childhood friend, Obiageli, visited her.

Adaku was critical of her husband. She felt that in a society where everybody was corrupt, was it not suicidal for her husband to be the odd man out? Were she and her children to suffer deprivation simply because her husband refused to do what others did with success? Surely she and her family were not going to be instrumental in reforming society. When society was ripe for reformation, then everybody would join in it. What was she going to tell her children when their neighbours bought new cars and colour televisions? Would she tell them that their father could not afford them because he had refused to take bribes? Her children would then ask her whether their neighbours took bribes.

Adaku was happy to see her friend. Obiageli had her own problems too but she had learnt to live with them, and had tried to cut out a personal life for herself, independent of her husband and children.

'You have not told me your problem,' said Obiageli.

'My problem,' she began, 'is my husband's attitude to me, and my children.'

Her friend smiled. She thought she had a greater problem; she had had five girls in a row and no son to carry on her husband's name. Her husband had told her that he did not mind, but she knew that he did. Her husband's friends had made jokes about her inability to produce a male heir. Her husband had not taken the jokes well. And besides, her husband's mother was already sick of the whole situation. She had moved to their home, and she was always reminding her son that he must have sons to carry on the family line.

Surely Obiageli's problem was much more serious than that of her friend, Adaku. But she had to encourage her friend to unburden herself to her.

'Does your husband beat you?' Obiageli asked. Adaku was horrified to hear her childhood friend ask this question.

'Of course not,' she answered. 'The day he beat me would be the day I leave him.'

Obiageli smiled. 'Have you thought where you

43

would go if you left your husband? You have seven children, and the youngest is only nine. Have you given a thought to it?' she asked.

Adaku looked blankly at her friend. She had never given a thought to it. Now she thought, where in fact would she go? To her parents, who had never sanctioned the marriage because her husband came from one of the remotest villages in the Rivers State? She had defied them and got married without their consent.

'I have never given a thought to this question,' Adaku confessed. 'But, you see, I am sick of his relatives. I have slaved for my husband and his relatives and what have I received in return? Nothing but insults and more insults,' she complained.

'Do they insult you in your own home or in their own homes?' Obiageli asked.

'All these questions, Obiageli! You don't seem to believe what I am saying to you. You think I am tired of my husband and looking for excuses to leave him? Perhaps you think I have found a brand new boyfriend . . .'

Obiageli laughed. 'No. Listen to me, I want to help you. I want to understand your problem. Forget all we said about marriage when we were at school. Remember we said we were not going to sleep with our fiances until the wedding night? What happened to us? Did we or did we not sleep with them years before we got married? Things have changed a great deal since we were children in school. We shall . . .'

'I know, Obiageli, but you see, my husband is so stingy. Apart from the food money, which is grossly inadequate, I have received no presents from him.'

'That is bad,' said her friend. 'Didn't he buy you presents when you had your babies? Surely he bought you laces for the christening of your babies. You have given him four lovely sons.'

Adaku began to cry. Her friend allowed her to finish, and as she wiped away her tears, Adaku continued. 'You see, he is very stingy. I slave for him, I wash his clothes and my children's. I iron them. I make do with whatever I have. I don't demand anything. Maybe that is why he takes me for granted.'

'If we must compare notes, I say to you, you have no problem. Your husband has never brought another woman into your matrimonial home, has he?' Obiageli asked.

'Never,' Adaku replied.

'I have seen girls brought into my home by my mother-in-law for my husband. When I objected, she reminded me that she had four sons, and said that if I did not like what she was doing, I should go back to my parents with my band of girls.

'If I was unlucky not to have boys, was it her son's fault or her own fault? I was merely taking after my own miserable mother, who had me and me alone. Oh, she was warned by everybody when her son was about to marry me. She should have heeded the warnings. But it was not too late. Her son would have wives and his home would be filled with sons and daughters.'

'What did your husband say to all this?' asked Adaku. She now understood her friend's problems.

'He said nothing. He did not protest. He did not reassure me either. He refused bluntly to have the matter discussed. So you can see how lucky you are.

You talk of stinginess. My husband denies me nothing. There was hardly a time he went abroad without buying lovely things for the children and I. I don't ask, but when I do ask for anything, he buys it for me. But you are better off. You have four sons and I have no son at all. We must count our blessings. We must thank God for big mercies, not for small mercies.' Obiageli paused before continuing, 'When I visited you a year ago, I told you to find time and see more of your friends. You learn a lot about life by meeting other people and talking with them. The problem with you then was that you were out of reality. You thought that if you left your family for a day, they would die. They would not die, they would learn to live without you. Sometimes they would not even miss you. So would you like to pay a visit to Anyaga next Sunday?'

Adaku agreed with pleasure, and looked forward to the visit. Anyaga was one of those girls who was over-sophisticated at school. She had announced in her second year at university that she was going to marry a doctor. Doctors were the craze at the time. Obiageli did not just want to marry a man who would be her friend and companion, she wanted someone who would love and respect her. As for Adaku, she had had no idea at all. All she said was that if her husband beat her, she would leave him.

Anyaga married her doctor all right, and there and then her problems began. The marriage lasted for only three years. Anyaga's sister-in-law made life so unbearable for her that her parents came and took her away.

Anyaga was now living as a single girl in Lagos. She had her son with her. Her husband's people

46

hated her so much that nobody made an attempt to ask for the boy. She had a very smart place in Ikoyi and her son attended a private school.

She was delighted to see Adaku. She and Obiageli met from time to time in Lagos.

'You have not changed a bit,' Anyaga said to Adaku.

'Oh, thank you,' said Adaku, feeling happy with herself. She had not been complimented on her youthful looks for a very long time.

'I mean it, Adaku,' Anyaga went on. 'You have not changed one bit and I hear you have seven children. You still comb your hair the way you did twenty years ago when we were at the University. You have gained weight in strategic places all right, but you don't look like the mother of seven grown up children. Look at me, all bones and no flesh. I nearly died when I had my only child. And you went through that ordeal seven times. You are great.'

'Adaku, you see?' Obiageli said. Then she turned to Anyaga and continued, 'When I visited Adaku a week ago, you would think that she had lost her husband or her mother. She complained of the stinginess of her husband, her crude in-laws and everything under the sun. She forgot to count her blessings. I told her my own story — five girls and no boy. She has four sons and three girls. Anyaga, do tell her your own story about before you left the matrimonial home. Then she will go home, embrace her husband and say, "You are the most wonderful husband in the whole world." '

What was there to tell? Anyaga was unfortunate to have married a very wicked man, who hated her as soon as they were declared man and wife. Unknown to Anyaga, her husband had had previous affairs which had produced three children, all boys. In fairness to her husband, he did not want to marry Anyaga. He did not love her. It was his sister who urged him to marry her. Anyaga was beautiful, well-educated and had a good job. The girl the doctor really wanted to marry had little or no education, and nobody really knew who her parents were. He kept protesting but his sister put her foot down. After all, did she not send her brother to England? Did she not arrange for his reception when he returned from England? Did she not even buy a car for him because the money the government gave for a car was too little for the brand of car the doctor wanted?

After the marriage, Anyaga's husband carried on with his affairs as if he was not married. He made no secret of them. When Anyaga protested, he beat her up, locked her in and went to work with the key in his pocket. Anyaga had three miscarriages before she gave birth to her only child, and it was by a Caesarean operation. While she was nursing the baby, there was a quarrel. Anyaga's husband beat her so badly that she fainted. Her husband, the doctor, left her to die. It was her nanny who phoned the hospital and they sent an ambulance to collect her. When she was discharged, her parents came to the hospital and took her away.

'My son is in a private school. I have a good job. To hell with husbands. I am a single girl with a son. I like my life. I don't go sleeping around, but I know whom I want to sleep with. The choice is mine. My job is full of challenges and I meet so many interesting people. I have had offers of marriage, but

I have turned all of them down. One marriage is enough in a lifetime.

'Do you remember Chiebonam?' she went on. Both women remembered her as one of the most fashion-conscious at the university. She always wore high-heeled shoes to lectures and never missed a single dance on campus. 'She is ill,' Anyaga announced, 'mentally ill. Man palaver. She came to my office the other day. I recognised her at once, in spite of the fact that she had aged and was dirty and unkempt. She told me she was in search of her children and asked if I had seen them.'

'No!' the women exclaimed.

'Yes, she said so. I was staring at her. I told her I had not seen them. Oh, she said, she had forgotten to tell me that she was married to that boyfriend of hers who wrote to her every week and sent her money and trinkets. Did I remember her boyfriend? I said I did not. Then she changed the subject. She was actually looking for a job in my firm. Could I introduce her to my boss? She could type, she could go on errands. In fact, there was nothing she could not do. It was with difficulty that I made her leave my office. I learnt later that she had escaped from the asylum!'

'Count your blessings, one, two, three. Count your blessings, four, five, six. Count your blessings and smile,' Obiageli and Anyaga sang. Adaku could not speak.

'What happened to Chiebonam?' Adaku asked.

'Well, what I heard from Isola, you remember her? She read classics at the University. She had a first class brain, won the coveted college scholarship and got a First in classics. You could not beat that. She was the first woman to gain a college scholarship and get a First Class. I'll tell you Isola's story later,' Anyaga went on. 'She told me that Chiebonam had two children. She became very ill during her third pregnancy. Her husband was abroad then. There were some complications, which sent her to the psychiatric hospital. Her husband returned, but refused to see her at the hospital because his relatives told him all sorts of stories about her. He did not investigate the stories and he just abandoned her. So she escaped from time to time from the psychiatric hospital and became quite a nuisance. Her husband got hold of her and banished her to the asylum.'

Adaku began to cry. She was a very soft-hearted girl and these disasters her friends had suffered hurt her. She was learning a lesson all right. Her visit to her own old friend was fruitful. She had learnt a lot. She was much better off than most of her peers. Why was she grumbling? Her husband had never raised his hand to strike her; he had never spoken an unkind word to her. Anyaga and Obiageli had told her of one of their classmates whose husband not only abused her during quarrels, but abused her parents as well. She began to doubt herself. Perhaps she was the cause of her problems and not her husband. How had she reacted to her husband's sexual demands of late? Was she not really in search of something which she herself did not know? What had made her so bitter of late? Her husband had always been stingy. Why was she reacting so strongly to this stinginess, sixteen years after their marriage? What was really wrong with her? Did she want a change? Of what? Of environment, of job, of husband? Perhaps that was it . . . a change of husband . . .

In the background, she heard Anyaga talking. She

hadn't finished. To hide her thoughts from her friends, as if they could really think her thoughts for her, or foretell her thoughts, she asked about Isola. Was Isola married? No, Isola was not married and had no children.

'What happened to her fiance at college? She had a very smart Efik boy who was very attentive. Didn't they get married in the end?' Adaku asked.

'They were married but you know Isola. She did not want anything noisy. She and her fiance quietly went to the registry one afternoon in Lagos and got married. The next day, her husband left for the United States of America. And that was the end of the marriage.'

'No.'

'That was the end of the marriage, I say. Her husband wrote a letter to say he had arrived in the States but gave no address. Isola wrote back, using the address of their mutual friend, and there the matter ended. No reply came from her husband.'

'She should have sued,' Obiageli said.

'You think Isola had time to go into all that?' asked Anyaga.

'Oh, but she should have married again. Such a lovely girl, such a brain,' Adkau lamented.

'That's life. So count your blessings, Adaku. The trouble with you is that you are very old-fashioned. Try to grow with the times,' Anyaga said.

To grow with the times, Adaku thought. What was the meaning of growing with the times? Anyaga was not the first person to say that to her. At her place of work, her colleagues had often told her that she was old-fashioned. She had laughed at them. If old-fashioned meant taking care of one's husband

and children, she did not mind.

But now she had begun to think and to think seriously. She had begun to ask questions she could not find answers to. She was surprised that these questions had persisted. Did she need another man in her life to help her cope with her frustration at home? How was she going to cope with that? A mother of seven children?

The women went on reminiscing, not about university days, but their school days. Their teachers didn't teach them the facts of life. They left so many things unexplained. They did not tell them that life was too complicated, and that they had to be taught to succeed. They were taught to turn the other cheek. That was all well and good in the time of Jesus, not in their own times. Turning the other cheek was cowardly, it meant bringing about your own end. It meant you were soft. The world was tough.

The women were taught to be humble. They remembered their good old teachers who were Oxford graduates, yet never in their six years in school did they show they went to Oxford. Nigeria especially did not want that. Nigeria was a place where you told everybody from the rooftops that you were a graduate or a holder of a doctorate degree. It would not do for you to sign yourself as mere Mr. or Mrs. You had to be Dr., Mrs. or Chief so and so. If not, people would not recognise your worth. You must wear your importance as you wear your shirt. When driving your car, if you were a doctor, you must have a piece of paper on which was printed "Doctor of Medicine" or "Doctor of Law" etc. Otherwise, if you had an accident, nobody would take you to hospital because you were an unknown. And, what's more, people would laugh at your humility.

At home, Adaku became a different person. Surely, all things considered, she was the most blessed of all her college friends. But she was determined that her life must change. She was not going to steal. She was not going to take bribes in her office. Oh, she could not do it. But she was going to live well. She was going to think more of herself.

So she went to the hairdresser and had her hair done. It cost her a fortune but she did not mind. She went to her wardrobe, got out all the dresses she had bought nearly ten years ago, washed and ironed them and took them to a charity home.

Then she went to a boutique and bought herself six smart working dresses which cost her over five hundred naira. She realised to her horror that her husband's stinginess had also affected her. She had not had a new dress for the past four years, yet she was saving. What was she saving for?

She wore one of the new dresses to work the next day, and everybody complimented her. 'That's a lovely dress,' her boss said. Adaku was on top of the world. Her boss had never before taken any notice of her. Suddenly everything became rosy, life became more meaningful. She knew within herself that she had changed. But she was not afraid of the change. She was rather excited. Soon, something great would happen to her.

A WIFE'S DILEMMA

Amma was daring. At first I thought he was merely being helpful and polite. Each time I came to his firm to inquire about something, he was very attentive. I was delighted. If you had been married for twenty years to a man who was very busy, who never complimented you on your dress or appearance, who never kissed you and never took you to a good restaurant to have a good dinner, then you would understand my admiration for Amma.

When I married my husband, I was told I was a very lucky woman. He was rich, handsome and responsible. We had six children, and we loved them, and gave them whatever they wanted; but we did not spoil them.

However, my husband became too busy as time went on. He became richer, less lovable and had no other interest apart from his business. I took care of the children and filled my time that way. But the last of the children went to a boarding school and I was left with nothing useful to do.

Then one day, my sister came to me and told me she wanted to start a laundry service in Lagos and that I should please help her buy the machines. My sister's husband was trained abroad in laundry services, but he had no capital to start up on his own. I could not deny my sister anything. I told my husband and he allowed me to go to Lagos. He also agreed to pay for the machines.

When my sister and I got to Cessel and Co. Ltd., the receptionist took us to Amma's office; and told him we had come to inspect some laundry machines which had just arrived from Germany. Amma quickly got up from his chair as we were being introduced. I stretched out my hand and he shook it politely. The receptionist left and my sister and I remained in Amma's office. We explained in detail what we wanted and he listened attentively to us. He gave us some brochures, and gave us another date to return to see more machines that were arriving in a few days time.

We left. At that time, I did not think much about him. He did not attract me in any way. But he impressed me as a very responsible person who was capable of rising quite high in his establishment.

'I am glad I came back just in time,' I heard Amma saying. You see I had gone to see him and he was not in his office. 'I went for my car. Oh and thank you for the letter,' he said.

'You received it?' I asked.

'Yes, only this morning. And I had a feeling that you would come today. Come let us go to my office.'

He shut the door, took me in his arms and kissed me fully on the mouth. I responded without any pretence at all. My husband kissed me only when we were courting. When we got married, he forgot all about kissing. If I tried to kiss him, he shut his mouth tight. I tried sometimes to take the initiative, but failed. So I gave up; and turned my attention to taking care of my children.

I enjoyed Amma's audacity. Well, he was in Lagos. Anything could happen in Lagos. He could talk to me and even want to flirt, only in Lagos. He could not do it elsewhere.

We discussed the business I came for. He had got all the information I had asked for in my letter. He wanted us to try other firms for the machines to find out whether there could be cheaper offers elsewhere. He knew his job. And I admire people who know their jobs. He had got brochures and studied them very carefully and made notes. So there was no beating about the bush.

'Your sister would like this one,' he said, showing me a brochure which I had not seen. 'She would have difficulty with the running of it though, because the maintenance cost would be too high. So it all boils down to buying ours. They are expensive, yes, but the running cost is minimal. We are here. We would service the machines and provide spare parts. But if you want to see the others, I am at your service.'

I wanted to see the other machines. Amma then excused himself and in a short time he came back looking a bit worried. 'I completely forgot,' he said, feeling rotten.

'Never mind, we shall take a taxi' I said. He scratched his head. A taxi? It was too expensive. I read his mind. 'And it is time for lunch too. Perhaps we should have something to eat on the way,' I said.

Amma came over to where I sat. Again he kissed me. I was in heaven. 'You don't mind going in a taxi?' he asked.

'Of course not. I came here in a taxi,' I said. We went outside, he hailed a taxi and we entered. 'We would have lunch, then go to inspect the machines. 'Where did you say they were?' I asked.

'Yaba,' he said.

'That's perfectly all right. I hope you won't be missed in the office,' I said.

The taxi took us to a restaurant. The place was nothing to write home about. I don't even remember the name. 'I shall have beer, while you eat,' he said.

'Please have something to eat. I must have lunch now, or my ulcer will . . ., well you know. Please eat something. Do you mind me paying? It's nothing at all,' I said.

What I did not know was that Amma knew quite a number of people in the restaurant. So when he excused himself and came back quite happy with himself, I was surprised. 'We are lucky,' he announced. 'I have found a car. I met a friend, I told him my problem, and he handed his key to me. So when you are ready, we will go.'

The car was a Beetle, and when I sat beside Amma I wondered when last I had sat next to a driver. When you were used to being driven by a paid driver, you will understand what I mean. It was all very romantic to me. All very fresh. Such simple joy which cost nothing. Amma apologised for driving me in such a car. He knew I had a Volvo and a paid driver. There was no need for the apology. It was rather exciting for me. I told him so. When he said that we were all alone in the world, I was as nervous as a girl of sixteen on her first date. Was I being desired by a young man? I was definitely much older than Amma. He took my hand and my heart missed several beats. How gorgeous. When last did I feel this way? Twenty years ago? Was I still capable of this kind of feeling? I had thought that that part of me had gone in the long years of my marriage.

'At last we are together, you and I,' he said. I wondered how many people realised how private sitting in a car with someone is.

'I don't know how to start, but please may I call you Chika?' he asked.

He must be civilized to ask that question. The days of chivalry were long gone in Nigeria, if they had ever existed. Where in Nigeria would you see a young man get up to allow an old man or woman to sit down, while he stood up?

The flyovers were endless. Those from the East who had very bad roads envied Lagos with her numerous flyovers. The flyovers had made Lagos dirty and almost uninhabitable. Lagos used to be a beautiful place. Now it was all slums and flyovers and the lagoon was fast disappearing. 'Do you think we can get along together?' Amma asked. I said nothing. He held my hand and went on driving. 'Do you think we can?' he asked again. 'Yes we can,' I said, my heart beating. To reassure him, I squeezed his hand and I think he was as delighted as I was.

It was a long drive and I said so. I wondered whether he would not be missed in the office. But he was not thinking of that. All he wanted was the success of our trip to inspect the machines. 'You know what,' Amma said. 'We might not meet the manager and this drive would be a fruitless one.'

'Fruitless?' I asked. 'Oh, aren't you enjoying my company? We are all alone in the wide world, you and I in this car. Was this a fruitless experience?'

'I am sorry. How dull of me, I never thought of it that way. How silly of me,' he said.

Then it began to rain. Thank God the wipers of the Beetle were in good condition. Amma drove very carefully in the rain. Then he suddenly asked. 'When did you say you were going back home?'

'As soon as this business is over,' I said.

'You can't be persuaded to stay a bit longer?' he asked.

'I am sorry, but I don't think so,' I said. 'I am sorry for all the trouble I have given you over these machines.'

'It is no trouble at all. Isn't it a romantic journey, driving in the Beetle in the rain, just the two of us as you said.'

We drove on in silence. It was still raining. I was wondering what was wrong with me. I had never behaved so outrageously since I married my husband. But Amma was a nice person. He was one of the nicest people I had ever seen. But how many did I meet? In my circumstances I met only my husband's business associates. They talked nothing but business and I was bored. Bored stiff. And what's more, my husband never realised how bored I was. And now this young man was sweeping me off my feet in this way. Where would all this take me?

At last we reached the place. The rain was still very heavy. Amma took great trouble to see that I was not wet and I was deeply touched. No amount of trinkets my husband bought me moved me in the way this did. He parked the car and joined me.

Just as we expected, the manager was not in, and there was nobody to show us the machines. In fact the manager had gone on leave and would resume duty in two weeks' time. The polite receptionist asked us to leave a message but Amma said not to worry, we would call again when he returned from leave. So we left.

Amma asked me to wait in the corridor while he went for the car. It was still raining and he did not want my beautiful hair to get wet. God bless him.

We drove away. The traffic was heavy and everywhere was wet and muddy. Amma seemed to know the area very well. To avoid the traffic we took a longer route and soon burst out at the highway. The rain had stopped now and Amma was driving very slowly. He was driving with one hand and holding my hand with the other.

Then he pulled up by the highway, stopped the car, took hold of both my hands and kissed me. I returned the kiss. Cars hooted and raced past. I didn't care who saw us. Then I heard Amma saying urgently, 'Shall we go somewhere? Shall we?' The voice was urgent and passionate. Then I heard a voice. It was the voice I had listened to all my life. I heard it clearly. The voice said, 'Chika hold it. Be careful. Be patient. Don't . . .' I smiled. And I heard Amma again, 'Shall we? Please, we can, you know.' Then he said other things which I did not hear. All I knew was that we were on the highway again, driving towards the restaurant where he would drop the car and I would then take a taxi to my sister in Surulere.

'You have said nothing,' Amma said. 'No, I must go to my sister now. We are going somewhere at eight o'clock.' Then in that case,' he said, 'I could get my car and come and see you at your sister's. Please don't say no.' I held his hand.

'I must go,' I said. 'There are many more days. I shall come back to Lagos again in a week or so. We shall see much of each other.'

'Well, there is nothing I can do now. You never know, I may die before you come back to Lagos again.' We roared with laughter at the joke. 'Don't joke with death in that way,' I said. 'I am so afraid of death. You know, before the war I gave no thought to death. I thought I was destined to live to be ninety.

60

I thought that only old people died. Then the war taught me that both the young and the old died. That in fact in wars only the young died and the old were left to bury themselves,' I said.

Amma thanked his friend profusely and we were faced with the big problem of getting a taxi. Normally when I came to Lagos without my car, I hired a taxi each day. It was much easier that way. The cost did not bother me at all. It was again romantic that Amma and I should stand by the road side, hailing taxis as they zoomed past.

We stood for ten minutes, and there was no prospect of getting a taxi. Amma suggested we took one of those dangerous 'Molues' to a junction where I could then get a taxi that would take me to Surulere. I was horrified. How could I been seen in such a vehicle? The 'Molues' drivers were nearly always drunk. During one of my visits to Lagos, one of the drivers of these vehicles stopped at the middle of the road. He climbed out, went straight to the open gutter, brought out his thing, urinated, put his thing back, then feeling very happy with himself, danced a few steps then climbed into his 'Molue' again.

Meanwhile motorists were on their horns, blaring as if the end of the world was near. They rained abuse on him. They told him he was a mother fucker and a bastard. He retaliated by refusing to move. We were there for thirty minutes until a policeman was called, who towed the vehicle away.

'I'd rather wait a little bit,' I said to Amma. Then it started drizzling. There was nothing I could do but take one of the 'Molues' because no taxi came. But the ones that came by were all filled to the brim, with

61

hands and legs hanging out.

As luck would have it, one stopped. We hopped into the front seat. It was dirty and the driver was equally dirty but he had a pleasant face and a sense of humour. 'Oga,' the driver said, 'why you henter dis motor? Or abi oga no get bread?' he joked.

'Bo, my broder you talk true. Oga no get bread o. Oga don broke,' Amma said.

'Ha, why, Oga no broke. Oga get bread.' They roared with laughter. What a country. Nigeria could be great when one thought of the people's pleasantness and easiness of manner and their readiness to see fun in everything.

'Big Oga,' someone said. 'You dey deceive us. You get bread. We want chop your bread,' the rest of the passengers laughed. It was all very entertaining. I rode in this type of transport twenty years ago. Up in my ivory tower, how could I know what went on underneath me?

We reached our destination, Amma paid and helped me down. The driver thanked Amma and the passengers wished us God speed. The junction could be seen from a distance and there were so many taxis along the highway. If we had waited outside the restaurant we could not have a taxi. I liked the way Amma did things.

Suddenly, a sense of loneliness overtook me. It had happened before, this sense of loneliness. It was when my first son left home for the first time. I had taken him to the school, and saw him settle in his dormitory. When it was time for me to leave, he said bye bye to me and before I knew what was going on, he had gone, and I was left alone. A week later, he lost his life in a gruesome accident.

So why this experience again? Here I was, with this beautiful man, who was showing me so much love, so much affection and respect, and then this sense of loneliness because he was leaving me and going to his wife.

I asked Amma if we could take a taxi to his office, collect his bag and then go to my sister's place. The taxi would then take him home. As I was saying this, he gripped my hand, crossed the highway and hailed a taxi. The taxi driver was willing to take us to Amma's office. It happened so fast that Amma was taken by surprise. At first he said nothing. Then he smiled at me and held my hand. 'I don't think I deserve all this affection from you,' he said. Before he said this, I was reading his mind. He was battling with himself. Should he accept this offer or not? After all, Amma was a Nigerian male. If he wanted a relationship with a woman of his choice, he wanted it on his own terms. He was not going to have a 'cash madam' mess his life.

But, he went on thinking, and I read it all, this one was not a 'cash madam'. This one had a lot more to offer apart from money. He wanted her company and besides, . . . no matter.

'As I was saying,' Amma continued 'I don't know why you should do all this for me. I could have easily taken another 'Molue' back to my office. But you see, well, I don't know. I cannot find words.'

We stopped a few yards away from his office, he jumped out of the taxi, collected his bag and we set out for Surulere.

'But I wanted us to go somewhere and you refused. We could still go somewhere,' he said.

'I was lonely,' I said. 'I remembered my son. I did

not want you to leave me alone in the taxi. If you left me with my sister, the loneliness would be less. Please understand,' I pleaded.

'I love to be with you Chika, make no mistake about it. It was quite an experience to be with you, to hold your hand, to kiss you, to talk with you. Maybe when you come back again to Lagos, we shall know more of each other. But, I could still come tonight. The day is still young.'

'I shall return,' I said.

Soon we were in Surulere. The taxi driver found my sister's place. I brought out some five naira notes and stuffed them in Amma's pocket before he had time to protest. 'Please don't bother to come out. I shall call on you in a fortnight or so. Please let me know about the machines by any means possible.'

Back home, it was not easy for me to go back to my normal schedule. There was that sense of guilt which I had never experienced since I got married. I felt that I was letting my husband down. How was I to behave when I saw Amma? Allow him to take me in his arms and kiss me? Give in completely when I was still living with my husband. Or avoid him completely, which meant not going to Lagos at all? Perhaps I should listen to the voice. But for days, the voice did not speak. It had deserted me.

While I was battling within myself, my sister's message arrived asking me to come to Lagos for the machines. So I was thrown into the business of getting ready for Lagos. But for one reason or the other, I was unable to leave for Lagos until five days after my sister's message. There were so many things to look into before leaving.

64

On the eve of my departure to Lagos, I was gripped with a kind of depression which I have never known before. I told my husband I did not feel like going to Lagos, that I was depressed and did not know the cause of my depression. He said it was nothing. 'Perhaps going to Lagos would make you feel better, you have been putting off going for sometime now, and your sister needs you.'

When I got to my sister's house in Surulere, I was told that she had gone to the market. So I took a taxi to Amma's office. His room was locked. When I asked about him, I was told he was in hospital. 'God don't let me faint here,' I begged God. My head was pounding. I could hear my heart beating. God, not in this place. I can faint in any other place, not here. So that was it. The depression. The loneliness. Amma was hale and hearty three short weeks ago. Amma must not die. He must not die, or else . . . or else I will die to. God, please . . .

Then I saw Amma's assistant. 'Good afternoon, madam. He is in hospital. He became ill a few days after your last visit. For some days, we did not see him. So our G.M. visited him. You know Amma is so nice to everybody. It was our G.M. who took him to hospital. He is much better now. I saw him yesterday. I was told he was responding to treatment. Thank God.'

I thanked the young man and dashed out of the building jumped into the taxi which was waiting for me and said, 'Take me to the Creek Hospital.' The taxi driver asked no questions. Soon we were there. I found the men's ward and went to the ward sister, and told her whom I wanted to see. But the ward sister was sorry, I could not see Amma. Only his wife was allowed to see him. He was very ill.

I told the sister that I was not his wife but that I wanted to see him for just five minutes. I had travelled nearly eight hundred kilometres to see him. The ward sister was sympathetic. She understood, and she asked me to follow her.

Amma was lying in the hospital bed, all bones and no flesh. 'Amma,' I called. 'It's Chika. I am back.' He turned his head and he smiled, a very sad smile. My heart sank. I gripped the edge of the bed Amma was lying on. By now, the sister had left us. 'Amma, it's Chika,' I cried. I must be courageous. I must behave properly. I took his hand. It was lifeless, without blood. It was the hand that was full of life and blood three weeks ago. Now it was lifeless. He smiled again. He recognized me. He wanted to talk, but no words came. But life was returning to the hand that I was gripping. His grip was tightening. I felt blood rising, I felt life. But Amma still did not or could not speak to me.

Then the sister came in. She watched us then she came nearer. She took my hand away from Amma's. She did it very gently, very solemnly, then she led me away through another door. 'His wife is waiting outside,' she said. 'Come again at nine o'clock if you want to. I shall be here.' I thanked her and left.

I was back at nine o'clock. I went straight to Amma's room, but he was not there. Fear gripped me. Then I saw the good sister. She took my hand and led me to her room. She gave me a seat and I sat down. She looked blank. I waited for her to say something. 'He is dead,' she finally said.

'Dead,' I repeated

'He died an hour after you left. I am sorry.'

'Thank you,' I said.

'We did everything to save him,' she said. 'It's God's will,'she continued.

'May God's will be done,' I said.

How would I mourn Amma? Wear black? Attend his funeral? See him lie in state? No. I couldn't see him as a corpse. After the funeral I would go and sympathise with his wife and children. Perhaps I should go to his home and see his parents and tell them that Amma was a beautiful son, that God had to call him, and what . . . what . . . and do what with him? He was so young . . .

MISSION TO LAGOS

Britain took the lead in sending thousands of professionals to lend technical assistance to Nigeria. John Hammer was a B.B.C. journalist who was sent by the British Council to teach at the newly formed Institute of Journalism.

Nigeria had just got her Independence and the developed countries of the West were eager to be in her good books. John Hammer came to Lagos with a kind of religious zeal to help Nigeria.

Things were not easy at first. There were problems of accommodation and the selection of students who would benefit from the course.

Eventually, he got accommodation in an old building that was adjacent to a brand new Institute of Management and Technology. The Registrar of this Institute was understanding and listened to Mr. Hammer's problems. When the latter called at his office, the Registrar told him he was welcome and he would be of assistance to him in any way possible.

It was not long after that Mr. Hammer called on the Registrar again and asked him whether he could get him a lecturer to teach the trainee journalists in African History. The Registrar could, and without hesitation, buzzed Yetunde Johnson who worked with him as an administrative officer. Yetunde came in and was introduced to John Hammer. They shook hands.

'She studied African History in the University of Ibadan under the tutorship of Professor Kenneth Dike. As they say in Nigeria, she will deliver the goods,' the Registrar said.

Yetunde said she was willing to take the students in African History and she and John Hammer agreed to meet and discuss the syllabus.

The assignment was a great challenge to Yetunde, who was not a teacher. It took her quite some time to go through the syllabus and prepare her lectures. When she got through preparing and giving the lectures, she was happy with herself. The students knew that she understood her subject and respected her.

The students told John Hammer how they enjoyed her lectures and tutorials, and he was pleased that he had made a good choice. The course was proving difficult for John Hammer. Communications were poor and books were not easily available. Most of the time he was not cheerful, and his students speculated about him. Then one day one of them asked him as a joke whether he had lost his wife.

John Hammer was startled.' No, I have not lost my wife,' he protested.

'Why then do you look as if you have? And even if you have,' the man went on, rather unkindly, 'there are other women. Lagos is full of them. Take your pick.'

John Hammer roared with laughter. And for the first time in six long months the students witnessed Mr. Hammer's laughter.

'All right boys, you win,' he said. 'Let's go to the "Centre" and have some drinks.' So they trooped to the Centre to drink beer with their director. He bought each of them a beer and was having one himself when Yetunde hurried in.

'Have you seen my boss?' she asked anxiously.

'No, we haven't seen your boss,' the men replied. John Hammer said nothing but looked at Yetunde as if he had never set eyes on her before. But she hurried out again amid protests of: 'Oh sit down and have a beer with us.' When she left, the students said very nice things about her. John Hammer listened but made no comments.

After her lectures one afternoon, Yetunde went to the Centre and saw John Hammer drinking alone and looking morose. 'Come on Mr. Hammer, the world is not coming to an end,' she teased.

'Sit down,' he ordered. 'I want to talk to you. Please don't be offended. But do tell me, are we welcome in this country? Is this course worth it? Are we wasting our time in this place? Does the public appreciate what we are doing?'

'What makes you think that we don't appreciate you in Nigeria?' Yetunde asked.

'You see this bunch of students, they just don't want to learn. They are over-confident. The boys have exaggerated opinions of themselves. They are not a bad lot, mind you,' he said.

'Well, do the best you can. You can't do more than your best. You will be surprised in the end, they will come up tops in their final exam. I agree with you that they are not a bad lot. But please stop calling them boys. They are not boys. They are responsible husbands and fathers. As a matter of fact, only five out of the twenty five of them are not married.'

'Oh thank you, Miss Johnson. I shall remember that,' John Hammer said.

'But do tell me, what makes you think we don't appreciate your presence here? It is not because of

70

the students and their over-confidence, is it?' Yetunde went on.

'Not exactly. I am sorry, but you see, well, I really don't know. I sometimes wonder why I am here, if the people I am supposed to direct know it all. That's what I mean.'

'They pretend that they do, being Nigerians. Your news media praise us to the skies. They say we are the hope of all Africa. They say we are the most populous, the most wealthy, the most stable. We have to act accordingly. We hate to be underrated,' said Yetunde.

John Hammer stared at her. She had a lot more to offer than he thought. He should not really be too patronizing. He should do his job as best he could and when it was accomplished take his leave. It was this lady who had brought this truth forcefully to him. He mustn't worry any more.

For weeks, John Hammer went to Yetunde's office just to see her face and to say hello. Then one day, he summoned enough courage to ask her out and she readily accepted.

He took her to a very expensive night club where they had a meal and danced. About midnight, he took her home, said goodnight at the door, and left.

They had gone out two or three times when John Hammer suddenly asked Yetunde whether she was ashamed being seen with him in public.

'Oh, good lord, no. Why?' Yetunde replied almost in protest.

John Hammer was reassured. The reply was not premeditated. It was truthful. 'Then would you like to go to a cocktail party with me tomorrow night?'

'Certainly,' she replied.

71

'Seven then. I shall come for you at seven.'

John was at Yetunde's at seven and, as they were driving away, John said, 'I am thinking of changing this car.'

'Why?' Yetunde asked.

'It does not become you. Too old for you.'

'Perhaps all you need do is put the clutch in order,' she suggested.

Yetunde was amazed at what John did about the car several weeks after. He had taken the car to be repaired and resprayed. It looked so new that she did not recognize it when she saw it. She wondered at men and what they did when they were infatuated. If they could move mountains, they would do so for a loved one. She was deeply touched and wondered where the relationship was leading her. She saw John getting more and more involved with her, and she enjoyed the involvement, yet had nothing to give in return. She hated to play games. She would lay all her cards on the table. She wasn't going to wait until it became too late.

They had gone to Bagatelle for a meal and when they were dancing Yetunde said to John, 'You haven't told me about yourself John. Isn't you wife coming here?'

John Hammer might have expected the question, but not at that particular moment, when he was in heaven, dancing with Yetunde.

However, he said to her 'Come let's go and sit down. We can talk better.' They sat down. 'The night I asked you whether you were ashamed to be seen with me, I had wanted to go further. But the reply I got from you made me so happy I couldn't . You see, I had thought you were ashamed of being

72

seen with me or that you might be technically married and all that.

'But to answer your question. My wife is not coming here. We have been at this for a long time. It has nothing to do with you. My wife has finally gone to live with her lover in London. The papers for divorce are filed, and I am now separated from her. Any time now, we will be free to go our separate ways.'

'And your children?' she asked.

'Oh, the boys, they are in good public schools in England. It's a pity they will grow up not knowing their father,' John said.

'Why should they?'

'I hardly see them. When I do, they tolerate me for an hour or so. You see, they see their mother more often than they see me. It makes all the difference.'

'Shall we go home now?' said Yetunde so abruptly that John showed surprise.

'Not now, please sit down. The night is still young. If we go now, I'll be very lonely in my flat. Please.'

They continued dancing. Then Yetunde began: 'I too was married and had a very nasty experience. My marriage lasted for only three weeks, and it was dissolved on the grounds of incompatibility. Luckily there was no child involved. But a year ago, I met someone whom I fell in love with. He is seeking divorce from his wife but my instinct tells me that he will not get it. So, here we are.'

They did not speak for a long time, but they danced on and, when the music stopped, it was John Hammer who wanted them to leave the night club.

It was only eleven o'clock when they arrived at Yetunde's flat. They sat down and for a while neither

73

said anything to the other. They now knew where they stood in their relationship. John Hammer was not disappointed at what Yetunde said to him. Somehow he believed that all would be well. Yetunde had said that she was not ashamed being seen with him. But there was a bigger problem apart from the one Yetunde had told him.

John Hammer was white and Yetunde was black. Yetunde's people frown on white and black relationships. True, Nigerian men had come back from abroad with white women as their wives. But it was still not common to see a black woman married to a white man. Yetunde was sure her people would not accept John Hammer.

'May I ask you,' John began, 'where this man is?'

'In London,' she replied.

'What is he doing in London?'

'Working,' she said.

'This may sound mean, but if he wants you as I do, he should come back to Lagos. He should leave his job. I can leave my job for you Yetunde, I know I can,' he said.

'I know you can,' she said.

'Thank you. You have made me so happy. You are my type of girl. You are four women in one,' John went on. Yetunde began to giggle.

'You are the gay woman; you are the serious thoughtful woman; you are the woman deeply interested in the politics of your country and also the culture — I mean the preservation of it. But what's more, you can be also a wife as well as a mistress.'

Yetunde laughed aloud. 'Thank you,' she said amidst laughter. 'But at which role do you think I excel?'

'I shall tell you later. I want you to be my wife, not my mistress, I am serious.'

Yetunde sat up now. She must stop this conversation before it got out of hand. 'Please, John, don't talk about marriage. It's not fair.'

'To whom?'

'To Dike,' she said.

'So that's his name,' he said.

'Yes, Dike is his name.'

'And what does the name mean? Your names always mean something,' he said. There was an element of mockery and of contempt in his voice, and Yetunde noticed it, but said nothing. That was the problem. For Yetunde had thought of this relationship much earlier on. She knew that apart from Dike, there was this obstacle. She had discussed it with her understanding boss who agreed with her, but advised her to be careful, and sensible. The relationship would lead her nowhere. If she agreed to marry John and they were sent to London by his organisation, what would she do? She couldn't go to London with him. She wouldn't want to live in London. And she wouldn't want to be an obstacle to John's advancement in his establishment. One had to think of all these complications before one took the plunge.

And Yetunde was no longer young. Her first marriage had opened her eyes to the uncertainties of female-male relationships. She was not going to make another mistake. John was in love now; she wondered what he would feel for her a year later. He liked many things in Africa now, but she knew that sooner or later, she would come up against his white superiority and during quarrels, for there were

75

bound to be quarrels, he would say nasty things to her. She would in turn say nasty things to him. They would both apologise, but the nasty and the unkind words would have been spoken. No, it was no use. John had to be told everything.

'You won't tell me the meaning of . . .' Yetunde heard John saying.

'For goodness sake John, please.' She was irritable, and John retreated to the balcony, and there watched cars as they drove past in an endless stream.

Yetunde went to the kitchen and made an omelette with six eggs. She had not known how to make an omelette before. It was John who taught her how. She made it now, sliced some bread and took it to the balcony where John was standing. Then she got a bottle of beer and water.

'Oh, and I have some lettuce,' she said, and got some lovely fresh lettuce and placed it before John.

'Thank you. You are a woman after my own heart. Sit down and eat with me,' he said. She ate a little, and said she was not hungry.

'Eat some lettuce then,' John said.

'You know I don't eat lettuce. I prefer our own vegetable which we eat raw. It is delicious with a kind of bitter sweet flavour. I can't find it in Lagos at all.'

'But you don't eat vegetables here at all.'

'That's a wild statement. How many homes have you visited in Nigeria to draw that conclusion? Go to the market and you will see forests of vegetables. Who eats them? Foreigners?'

'There you go again. I didn't mean any harm. It was just an observation. If I had my way, I'd eat all my food raw.'

76

'You will do whatever you like. Here only goats eat their food raw. I went to a restaurant in London. I was asked how I wanted my steak, and I said well-done. The waiter thought I said half-done. So when he brought my steak I couldn't eat it.'

Then Yetunde wondered what food she would prepare for John if they were man and wife. As a wife, she would take care of his meals. She hated foreign foods. John had pretended he liked egusi soup the first time he tasted it. He even ate with his fingers. Would he continue to enjoy egusi soup and other Nigerian foods? Would our food upset him?

John joined her in the kitchen now while she was washing up the plates. He dried the plates for her, then held her close and kissed her very tenderly. 'There was a time I thought you did not kiss anyone,' John said, and Yetunde roared with laughter.

'You think all sorts of things, John. Well, it's one of those bad things we learnt from your people. Kissing is not hygienic.'

'I know it's not. But you're in heaven when it's happening to you.' And they kissed again.

'As I was saying,' Yetunde began. 'Dike is not the only obstacle. As I told you, my feminine intuition tells me that he will not get his divorce. But you and I cannot make it as husband and wife. The sooner we accept this obvious fact the better. I don't want to appear a fraud. Please understand me. There are too many things against us.'

'I know, I know. But things have changed. We are in the mid sixties you know. God knows I didn't come to Nigeria to marry a Nigerian woman. God knows, I tried as much as possible not to fall in love with you. But here we are. I have never met anybody

half as good as you are. You have a tremendous hold
on me. God, my friends in London would never
believe that here in Nigeria I had fallen desperately
in love with a Nigerian woman, and she is in love
with somebody else. Yetunde, I tried not to. But
there it is. I am concerned about you. I hope Dike is
worthy of you. It's not your fault for being you. Why
are we what we are? Why do I love you? Why should
you be you?'

She got up, and he followed her. He kissed her
again and again. 'You can see I can't help myself.
You have made me very happy.'

'It's one in the morning, John.'

'Yes, I know. I have six more hours to be with you
. . .'

Yetunde's boss was talking to her in the office when
John Hammer was announced. The boss asked him
to come in. They shook hands and the boss told
John he was tooking very well, that he had not seen
him so cheerful before.

'It's all her doing,' John said, and Yetunde nearly
collapsed. They discussed his business and he went
away.

Yetunde always listened to her boss's advice. 'So?'
he said. Yetunde smiled. 'I told him it won't work.
But he said he couldn't help himself.'

Her boss, a man of fifty four, with six lovely
daughters understood. 'The relationship is good for
you. You already know that it is hopeless waiting for
Dike's divorce. Nothing will happen in the next four
years when he does file his papers. So don't worry.
You are about five years older than my first
daughter, so what I tell her, I also tell you. The

relationship will not do you any harm. Have an open mind about it all.'

On Sunday, Yetunde and John drove to Badagry for the day. They found a secluded place near the sea and they had a picnic there. It was not till the evening that they drove back to Lagos.

Back in Yetunde's flat, John observed, 'So you see, Yetunde, we stayed together all day. We drove to Badagry, we bought fruit and vegetables on the way, we called on friends. We came back, you cooked a delicious meal. We talked, we worked, and not one cultural conflict. So you see, you are exaggerating the cultural aspect of our relationship. If we say it does not matter, then, it does not matter.' Yetunde said nothing. After the meal she dozed off in the chair. John lifted her gently from the chair and took her to bed. Then he kissed her; and said her body was smooth.

'The thing about you is that you have everything in the right proportion. Oh, you are good for me.' He began to kiss her again, covering her body with kisses, sending electric-like currents all over her.

Then he said, 'Your blouse will be crushed, let me remove it.' Then he removed her ear-rings and watch and chain. 'You have so much jewellery. Of all my women, you have the most expensive jewellery; and the most sophisticated.'

They lay in bed and talked about Lagos, about the people they worked with, about the books they had read.

'You seem to get on well with the people you work with,' John said. 'How do you do it?'

She smiled. 'My boss taught me that trick. I try to understand them, then I pay them compliments even when they don't deserve them, and above all, I help them solve their own problems if I can.

'I have also learnt to be diplomatic in my dealings with people.'

Yetunde appreciated this relationship so much because with John Hammer, there were no dull moments. He was a resourceful person. He was always making things, constructing miniature boats and trains. He even Made Yetunde a lovely tray which she cherished very much. With John, she was safe. With Nigerian males it was quite a different matter. All they wanted was sex and nothing more — well, those she had had the misfortune of meeting. John came and put new life in her and her intellect was sharpened.

Then he began to kiss her again. But she did not want that. She did not seem to be responding to his caresses. 'Oh, Christ, Yetunde, even here there is a barrier. Why can't you give? Tell me what you are thinking of and I'll tell you what has just come to my mind.

'It is amazing how the mind works. I suddenly remembered this woman I met in Ghana five years ago. She was well educated, M.A. and all that. We met at a party. Out of boredom or something, I invited her out for a weekend. She accepted and we went out of town. Well, the weekend was very successful. Everything went well. My wife was away in London so she moved into my flat and we lived together for eight months. But I was not in love with her. Our relationship was on a physical level. There was nothing emotional about it.'

'And here we are naked in bed and we can't make love. It is amazing and you talk of your woman in

Ghana and you talk of barriers and . . .'

'Please let me explain.'

'And you blame me for not giving when you have just confessed about this Ghanaian woman. John, I like you a lot, I want you just as a friend, not a lover or as a husband. You make me do a lot of things. You inspire me a good deal. I have appreciated our relationship very much. I want our relationship to be on this level, not the level you want. And besides, I don't attach too much importance to physical relationships, I mean, sex and all that, and . . .'

'Please, allow me to explain . . .' pleaded John.

'I don't want you to get hurt. I know that if I allow things to go the way you want them to go, you will get hurt. Can you imagine me living in London with you? Me so nationalistic and . . .'

'Why not? London is international. You will enjoy London very much. It is a place I love. I'll make you love London.'

'No thank you. London is not for me. Lagos is my home,' said Yetunde.

'I know you love Lagos. If you want me to leave this job tomorrow, I'll leave it. The mind works in a mysterious way. This Ghanaian woman came to my mind, I don't know how. Please forgive me. The excitement, the fact that we are together, naked in bed is too much for me and has temporarily rendered me impotent, so to say.'

Yetunde was touched. She kissed him and held him close to her. Surprisingly enough, they fell asleep. When they woke up, they made love.

The next morning, at the office, Yetunde heard John's voice. She smiled. John was a quiet person, one rarely heard his voice. Now he was almost shouting good morning to everyone in sight. Then he walked into Yetunde's office.

'Good morning my love, here is something special for you. Tell you what, the boys, I mean the men asked me if my wife had had a baby boy!' He roared with laughter.

'Yes, you behave as if she had,' Yetunde said quietly. 'You are wearing a new suit, a new tie, a new pair of shoes. You are celebrating?'

'Yes, you have made me very happy. I am hosting the men at the "Centre" this afternoon. Care to join us?'

'No thank you . I have work to do.'

'Okay, see you tonight.' He was gone.

Yetunde opened the parcel. A gold chain was delicately entangled in the stem of a red rose. It was so cleverly done that the thorns of the rose did not injure the chain. Excitedly, her hands shaking, she disentangled the chain from the thorns of the rose and examined it carefully. It was solid gold. She smiled, put the chain back and telephoned John.

'Thank you for the gift,' she said. 'It's very beautiful.'

'Oh it's nothing,' John murmured.

'You shopped this morning?' she asked.

'This morning, and all my money is gone.'

'John,' she said, 'my papers are through for the trip to London. I can leave any time now.'

'Oh, so soon, well, I'll see you tonight.'

That afternoon Yetunde received a strange letter from Dike which said that they had to call it quits. Yetunde was free to love anyone she cared to love.

He had thought over the whole matter and he had come to the conclusion that the sooner they knew where they stood, the better, to avoid being hurt.

Yetunde took the letter to her boss and burst into tears. Good man that he was, he consoled her. It was better now than later. There should be no regrets. She was free now to think about John.

When she came to her room, her telephone was ringing. She picked it up. It was John. 'I am coming right away,' he said.

'I have good news. My organisation want me back in London in four weeks' time. The big boss said I had done a good job. This is very rare in our establishment. The big boss never compliments anyone. I have succeeded. You are partly responsible for my success. Oh, be my wife, please. Here, read the letter,' and he threw the letter in the air and it landed on her table.

'Congratulations,' Yetunde managed to say.

'As I said, my papers are through for the trip to London. The course lasts for six weeks. If all goes well, I should be in the United States for another six weeks.'

Later in the evening, they discussed his travels. Yetunde would meet him there. She could not bring herself to tell John about the letter she received from Dike. There was no need. She and John were going to London. Perhaps she would be disposed to marry him. It was a possibility. But right now, she was confused. She wanted to be left alone to sort herself out.

THE CHIEF'S DAUGHTER

'My daughter will marry no one,' the Chief said. The Chief's wife laughed aloud. 'Our father, you are merely joking. You do not mean it.'

'My daughter will marry no one, Uloma, I have said this several times. I am not joking. I don't joke with women. You know that very well. When Adaeze returns from the land of the white people, she is going to stay here, right here with me. I have provided her with everything. She is one of the directors in ten of my twenty companies. She will receive a director's fees every month from the companies, I have already seen to that. Her house is waiting for her. I have furnished it to her taste. She in fact went with me to Milan to choose the furnishings. So you can see, I have arranged everything,' the Chief concluded.

'Our father, so you said. But you don't reckon that right now she might have one or two boys hovering around her. Adaeze is a beautiful girl, you know. She has been away from us for six years. She must have changed. True she has always been fond of you. But remember, even before she left for the land of the white people, you used to have violent exchanges. Of all your children, she was the only one who would stand up to you and disagree with you. So whatever arrangements or plans you are making for her, make sure that she is in favour, otherwise you will be very disappointed. If her mother were alive, it would be quite a different matter, but as it is she is no longer with us and you know that . . .'

'Uloma, that will do. Adaeze is not your daughter, she is my daughter, the daughter of my favourite wife. Just as her mother obeyed me in all things, so will Adaeze obey me in all things. I spoke to her when I was in London. I told her my plans for her. She listened, and said nothing. And as you know, silence means consent.'

'Our father, this may not be so. You were far away from home. You had gone over there to be treated. She did not want to upset you. That was why she was silent. When she returns home, you will see. Make allowances for her, or else you will be disappointed.'

'I have heard you, now out of my presence. I don't know how you thought you could tell me what to do. Adaeze is my daughter. She will do what I want her to do. She will marry no one, I say.

Uloma took leave of her husband and the Chief was alone. Adaeze was the Chief's first daughter, whose mother he had loved and admired. She died prematurely having her second child. The Chief had many wives but few children. His people said he was not blessed with children. His 'chi' gave him wealth but did not give him plenty of children. This lack of many children did not bother the Chief too much. Surely, he thought, ten children between four wives was quite a good number for him though other Chiefs like him had up to twenty five. What really bothered him was that none of his four sons showed signs of ever carrying on his businesses after he was gone.

It was only his beloved Adaeze who proved, if proof was needed, that she was the offspring of the Chief. She was every inch her father. She was so like him that the Chief kept asking his 'chi' why it did not make her a man so as to replace him. Adaeze was as intelligent as her father, hard-working and industrious. Before she went abroad, when she was home on holidays, she was always with her father. She took interest in his business and she offered advice, which though sometimes childish, impressed the Chief so much that he was very proud of his Adaeze.

The Chief did not understand what Uloma was saying to him. Surely Uloma his dear wife was not a stranger in their village. Surely she did not go to school, so she was not spoilt by the so-called Western Civilization. Surely she knew that it was the practice in their native land for a favourite daughter to remain at her father's home married to no one, but to have children who answered her father's name. Surely this custom was still carried out in their village in spite of the missionaries and their strange ways.

The Chief's mind went to the missionaries who taught them how to read and write. He chuckled to himself when he remembered their religion. How ignorant they were to think that it was their religion that brought his people nearer to the white missionaries. Their religion had nothing to do with it. It was the education they offered that made the Chief's father send his son to school. Their religion was strange. Imagine loving your enemy and doing good to those who hated you. The accepted thing was to hate your enemy and wish him dead.

The Chief remembered his childhood friend who died before he had a child by his wife. His sister supported his widowed wife, and she in turn stayed and bore sons and daughters for her husband who was long dead. His friend could not just die like that and his name die with him. His sister did the best thing a sister could do.

Then the Chief's mind went to his four sons, and he shook his head in regret. Why did fate treat him so? He thought of his first son. He was only ten when the war broke out. They had fled from Onitsha to a refugee camp when the Federal troops overran Onitsha. He had found it extremely difficult to keep track of his son. His mother was not of any help because she was too busy with the 'attack trade' to know where her son was or what he did. So unknown to them, the Chief's son disappeared. Nobody knew where he went. The Chief went from one refugee camp to the other in search of him. It was after five days that he was told that his ten year old son had joined the army and was in fact the batman of a Major who was fighting at the Onitsha war front.

The Chief knew all the service chiefs in the army. So it was easy for him to retrieve his son and bring him back to the refugee camp where they were all staying. The other sons were equally unruly, and when the war ended, none of them went back to school. The Chief tried to make them see reason, but they had all turned a deaf ear. So he let them be, and concentrated all his attention, and love, on his first daughter, Adaeze.

What then was Uloma telling him? Who was Adaeze's father? Surely he was. He sent her abroad. She would do what he wanted her to do. She would marry no one.

Soon it was time for Adaeze to return home. Her fiancé was already home and they had agreed that he would go to her father and ask for Adaeze's hand in marriage. Ezenta, Adaeze's fiancé was a good man who was genuinely in love with Adaeze. He knew the problem and determined to solve it. So when he returned, he told his own parents about Adaeze. His mother would not hear of it. 'No, my son, you are not going to marry the daughter of Chief Onyeka. The Chief wants to marry his own daughter himself. So please let us look for another girl for you. I have been thinking of the daughter of Chief Ezeora, you know her? She is not an illiterate. She is most suitable. I have confided in her mother and she was thrilled. Please forget about the daughter of Chief Onyeka. He is a difficult man. She would not do. We would be in serious trouble if we went for his daughter, please my son.'

Ezenta's father was not as opposed as his mother. He was an easy going man who treated everyone on his merit.

'We should not visit the sins of the father on the daughter, my wife,' he said. 'And remember how opposed your own father was to our marriage. The children are young, let them handle their own affairs themselves.'

'Ezenta's father,' Ezenta's mother said. 'You know the Chief very well. You know how powerful he is, so please let us persuade our Ezenta to turn his attention to someone else. The Chief has had a lot of problems. Look at his sons. How many of them is he proud of? None. He wanted to make his daughter his son. Nobody is quarrelling with that. It is an old custom of our people. But we should talk our Ezenta out of the whole thing that's all.'

And so there was opposition on both sides. Ezenta had to travel back to England to report to Adaeze that he had not made any headway with his parents, not to talk of her own father, the Chief, who did not even want to see him.

So Adaeze and Ezenta got married quietly in London and Adaeze went home to confront her father.

The Chief was happy to see her, but he did not like the way she came back unannounced. Surely if his daughter were away in England for over six years, he should tell the whole world that she had returned with the golden fleece. There would be a big party for her and a big thanksgiving service. Adaeze had spoilt everything by coming home like a thief.

'What do you think you are doing?' he asked Adaeze after embracing her.

'Papa, please. I know you like noise, I don't like noise. You know that things like this don't appeal to me at all.'

'Things like what?' the Chief asked.

'Like thanksgiving and parties and all that.'

'Hee, say that again Adaeze, say that again. Aren't you my daughter? Am I supposed not to make merry when my own daughter returns from the land of the white people? Did I send you to the land of the white people so that you would steal into my compound unannounced. Was that . . .'

'Our father, it is enough. It is enough. Our father, you must realize that Adaeze is a mere child. She does not understand. She has lived in the white man's land for a long time, and so she should be taught gradually how to behave as our people do. Adaeze,' Uloma said, turning to her. 'Come, my daughter. Come to my apartment. You are like a child. You should have sent us word that you were

89

coming home. Our people don't behave in the strange ways the white people do. Your father is angry with you. Come with me. Come and rest. Soon your father will be calm again, and we can talk.'

The following Sunday, there was a Thanksgiving service in the local church. Chief Onyeka sent out hundreds of invitations to friends, relations and well wishers. Cows were slaughtered and the people made merry. Everybody was impressed with Adaeze. The pastor who delivered the sermon was particularly pleased because not only had Adaeze returned with the golden fleece, but she had returned single. Adaeze was not like other girls before her, who forgot where they came from because they were privileged to go to the land of the white people. The pastor referred to those wrong-headed girls who unknown to their parents got married overseas. He wondered who gave them away. It was a shame that they forgot the customs of the people, and behaved as if they had no homes.

Adaeze, the daughter of Chief Onyeka, had proved a shining example for all the boys and girls of the whole clan to emulate. He wished the family well. He prayed that God should give Adaeze a good husband worthy of her, who would respect and love her . . .

The congregation forgot that they were in church. They began to clap. Adaeze could not help smiling to herself. She was not particularly happy about the thanksgiving service. But her father's wife, Uloma, had persuaded her to go, because it would please her father. Her father's wife had brought out some beautiful 'gorge' for her with matching lace blouse and headtie. But Adaeze in her strange way, would have none of that. She came to church, such a big occasion, in a two piece dress with a funny hat. Her cousins, and she had plenty of them, were most unhappy about her outfit. So as soon as the service was over, they went straight to her father's wife, and demanded to know why they were not told that Uloma had no 'gorge' to give to Adaeze to wear, but must allow her to appear in church in such an atrocious attire. Uloma knew her in-laws well enough not to be offended. She explained to them and they shrugged their shoulders. If Adaeze wanted to appear in that shabby outfit, that was her funeral, not theirs.

Meanwhile, Chief Onyeka was in the vestry castigating the pastor for his sermon. Had he never heard that his daughter Adaeze would marry no one? Had he never heard that there was nobody in the entire clan who was good enough for his daughter? The bewildered pastor apologised profusely and the Chief stormed out of the vestry.

In the evening when the merriment was over, Chief Onyeka called Adaeze to his bedroom and sat her down. He reminded her of their conversation when he was in London. He told her that he was serious. That he had made her a director in his numerous companies and that he would provide for her and her offspring. So . . .

'My offsprings who would be bastards?' she queried.

'Will you keep quiet. You are my . . .'

'I will not keep quiet, I am your daughter, all right. I am not a bastard. You married my mother, didn't you?'

'Will you keep quiet, I say or . . .'

'Father, I demand to know whether you married my mother or not. I am not your wife, I am not your son. I am only a girl, your daughter, and if I don't marry Ezenta, you have lost me forever. You will not see my face again. I shall disappear from the face of the earth. I shall kill myself and kill you, I shall oh . . . Come over here, my father's wife. Come, my father wants me to be a prostitute. Was my mother a prostitute? Didn't my father marry her the traditional way? What kind of custom does my father want to practise? Tell me, tell me, my father's wife, for I am confused. I am lost. I am . . .'

Everybody in the clan heard of the quarrel between father and daughter. The Chief's wife, Uloma, thought she must act or else there could be bloodshed. She knew her husband very well. She knew that he would never say yes to any man who wanted his daughter's hand in marriage. The Chief could not bear to see Adaeze the wife of anyone be he a millionaire's son or the President's son.

So she went to Chief Ezeora, the childhood friend of her husband. The Chief was in when she arrived.

'*Eze Uri*,' Uloma greeted him.

'*Odoze aku*,' the Chief replied. 'You are so early. I hope all is well.' He knew of course that all was not well. He had heard of the violent quarrel between his friend and his daughter.

'All is not well, our father. Your friend wants to marry his own daughter. Please come and put sense into him. Tell him that times have changed. Tell him that he sent Adaeze to the land of the white people to improve herself and all of us. That he did not send her there to behave like us in this clan. Tell him to allow her to marry whom she wants to marry.'

The Chief cleared his throat. He thanked Uloma for coming to see him. He too had tried like a friend to convince his friend that what he had planned for his daughter was difficult for her. He had told him that if he were not careful, that he would lose his daughter for ever. The Chief promised to see his friend again.

Both Chiefs exchanged greetings in the usual manner and went straight to the problem. Adaeze's father said he could not bear to see Adaeze get married. He wanted her to take care of his home, and that was that.

Adaeze was called. She knelt before her father and his friend. She appealed to her father to let her go.

'Please let me go. I am already married to Ezenta. We married in the Registry and I am expecting his baby,' said Adaeze.

'Now you are talking. That's exactly what I want, a baby. You will have the baby in this house, and he will be my baby. Marriage in the Registry? That can be taken care of. There is no problem at all. This is exactly what I want. I did not say you were not to have children. I said you would marry no one. No husband would care for you the way I would care for you. Please stay with your father,' Adaeze's father pleaded.

Chief Ezeora interrupted. 'Listen, my friend. Your daughter has said that she is already married to Ezenta. Don't you know Ezenta? I begged you to see him when he came from the land of the white people, but you refused. They are now married. That is what your daughter is saying to you.'

'And that is exactly what I am saying. Marriage in the Registry? Nonesense. I can take care of that.'

93

'The marriage was in the land of the white people, not in Nigeria, and you can do nothing,' said the Chief's friend.

'Try to understand me, my friend,' Adaeze's father continued. 'If you say, you are not well, you are not. Adaeze will say that she was not married in the Registry. That is that. There is no problem.'

'If her husband took offence and took her to court?'

'You are now talking. There are lawyers. Marriage can be dissolved any day. I'll take care of that.'

'And if I say no?' Adaeze said. She was boiling with anger. She was beginning to dislike her father. She used to be very fond of him when she was a child. To her, in those childhood days, her father was solid and powerful, he did no wrong. Anybody who got on the wrong side of her father deserved it. Her father was upright, he was just. He was her father, so he had to have these qualities.

Therefore like the true daughter of her father, she had inherited his stubbornness and his iron-will. But, her education abroad had taught her that she must play her cards well. She must not confront her father. Nobody, she remembered from her childhood days, who confronted her father, ever got what they wanted. So she was not going to use confrontation to fight her father. She would use her commonsense, her education and her charm.

So she apologised and said instead, 'I understand you my dear father,' she said. 'I did not mean it when I said that I was married to Ezenta. I could not have done such a foolish thing without your consent. You should have asked me who gave me away. And my dear father . . '

94

'Exactly, my daughter. Didn't I say you were my devoted daughter. That was why I treated the registry nonsense the way I did. I knew you were merely pulling my leg. You are every inch your mother. She was a delightful creature. She was always pulling my leg. She had a tremendous sense of humour. My friend, you have heard my daughter. You can take your leave so that father and daughter can talk in confidence.'

Chief Ezeora, of course, understood from Adaeze's eyes. The Chief was autoratic in his arrogant ways; he did not know that he was being fooled by no other person than his beloved daughter.

The following weeks were spent by father and daughter in the latter's office. The Chief was teaching Adaeze. He showed her the books that were kept for different businesses; the businesses that made profit and so on. Adaeze was intrigued. She asked questions that pleased her father. She made suggestions which her father jumped at and implemented forthwith and got favourable results therefrom.

But Adaeze thought of a way to escape from the clutches of her father. Besides, her pregnancy was developing fast. Soon, she would be unable to follow her father on his numerous tours.

The opportunity came when her father travelled to Kano. She confided in her father's wife, Uloma, who was afraid of the Chief's wrath when he returned. In just under twenty four hours after her father's departure to Kano, Adaeze was with Ezenta in London. In a matter of days, they had left London and left no forwarding address.

'Is my daughter in?' the Chief inquired as soon as he returned from Kano.

95

'Let me see, our father. Welcome home, our father,' Uloma said. She was always there when the Chief was around. Other wives did not show their faces when the Chief was around. If he wanted them, he sent for them.

'Our father,' said Uloma 'I cannot find Adaeze. She was here a while ago. Shall I bring you something to drink? Adaeze will be back soon.'

'Can't you ask someone to look for her. You said she did not go far. And here, here is my briefcase, take it to the room. I have money in it. And now . . . who is there? I never see anyone to do anything for me when I come to my own home. Where is the driver?'

'Our father, you asked him to go. He has gone,' Uloma said.

'Have you asked someone to look for my Adaeze, woman?'

'Someone has gone, our master. Sit down and take it easy. You have just returned from a far place. You are tired. Drink something, put up your feet on the cushion and relax.'

'While I wait for Adaeze?'

'Yes, my master, while you wait for your beloved Adaeze,' Uloma said.

But Adaeze didn't come. The Chief was alarmed. He went to Adaeze's room and found it empty of Adaeze's possessions.

'Where is my daughter?' he shouted. The whole household was frightened. All knew what had happened but none wanted to be a scapegoat. The Chief received no answer. 'Am I not in my own house? Uloma, where are you?' But Uloma had long disappeared from the scene. The Chief then under-

96

stood.

The driver had gone. All the Chief could do was take the car to the airport. He must stop his daughter. He found his keys. He jumped into the car, put the key in the ignition. The car would not start. When did he last drive himself? He could not remember.

He removed the key. He opened the door of the car, got out, went to his room and wept. Uloma came in, knelt before him and said, 'Our father, times have changed. Adaeze is your daughter, you sent her to the land of the white people. She went there and learnt their strange ways. You have not lost her. She is still yours. Try and understand her, she can still be very useful to you, because she is a good woman like her mother. She is still the Chief's daughter.'

ALPHA

Nobody knew Alpha so well as Tonia. They had met at a dance several years ago. Alpha was working and Tonia had just left school and was an applicant. Alpha was not very fond of dancing, but he went to that dance at Aba and there he met Tonia. 'Will you dance with me?' Alpha asked Tonia. She giggled, said something to the girl who sat with her, and got up and danced. Alpha danced very well and Tonia enjoyed the dance. 'Come with me to my table,' Alpha invited. And without hesitation Tonia and her friend followed him.

He bought them drinks and ordered five chickens. The girls began to giggle again. They whispered something and laughed aloud. Alpha was upset. 'If you don't want the chickens, I'll throw them away,' he threatened. The girls recovered immediately. That was crude behaviour they thought. What was wrong? What did he think he was doing, bullying them in that way as if he had known them for years? Tonia's friend was apprehensive but Alpha's behaviour amused Tonia and she was prepared to have a very good laugh that night. After all, the night had been rather dull before Alpha asked her for a dance. This was a way to brighten up everything before they went home.

'Eat the chickens then,' Alpha said, 'and please, I don't want anybody to dance with either of you.'

'Ewoo' exclaimed Tonia's friend. 'You sure are bossy. Good luck to you Tonia. I am going back to my seat. See you in the morning,' Tonia's friend left.

'Three is a crowd,' Tonia heard Alpha saying.

'No thank you, the lady does not want to dance,' he said to someone who knew Tonia and had come along to ask her to dance. The fellow went away with Tonia's friend.

'What a guy,' he said to Tonia's friend. 'We have all sorts in Nigeria these days,' Tonia's friend said, and told him what happened a few minutes before.

'But you did not come with him?'

'No, we did not.'

'Why this possessiveness then?'

'Perhaps he has made it,' said Tonia's friend.

'So he has bought Tonia with chickens! My, there must be other ways of making a girl yours. This is rather crude.'

'It's the Nigerian style,' Tonia's friend said.

Meanwhile Tonia and Alpha were now dancing again. 'You are a good dancer,' Alpha said.

'Thank you,' Tonia replied.

'You must be in school,' said Alpha, trying to make conversation.

'I am in school.' Tonia did not want to say which school. In those days, you just did not meet a man and give him all your life history. You played some pranks, like giving him a false name and address, or just not giving him any name at all.

'And your friend?'

'Yes we are in the same school.'

'What school, if I may ask?'

Tonia told him. 'That is a good school, I know somebody who attended it. There used to be a very interesting missionary in that school, is she still there or has she gone?' asked Alpha.

'I know the one you mean. She has got married.'

'No, you are joking.'

'We were all surprised, of course, when we heard that she was married. She met this man on her way back to England by boat, and by the time they arrived at Liverpool, they were engaged. Two weeks after, they were married. She told us all about it in her letter to the whole school. It was a great surprise to us that she could talk like that of the man. Hitherto, we did not know that the missionaries could marry. We learnt a lot from her.'

They danced on and on, and Alpha was really getting interested in this girl, Tonia. 'Would you like me to take you out next Saturday?' he asked

'Yes, of course.'

Next Saturday found Alpha and Tonia at the night club again. This time Tonia's friend was not there. They talked a lot and danced.

They saw a lot of each other until Tonia went back to school. Then they exchanged letters, and during the next holidays, Alpha suggested that Tonia should come home with him and be introduced to his mother.

'Does your mother live with you?' Tonia asked.

'Oh no, she is only visiting. But she would like to see you. She wants to see as many of my girlfriends as possible before she finally makes her choice.'

'She makes her choice?' Tonia did not quite get that.

'Yes, I am single. My mates have all married. Mother is worried — perhaps she thinks I am a eunuch or something dreadful. I tell her that I am choosy, that the girl I really wanted to marry has

100

married someone else, and that as long as she is alive, I am not going to be truly happy in marriage.'

That was intriguing. Tonia was quite an adventurous girl. She wanted to find out all about this man who called himself Alpha.

'I am intrigued by your name. Who gave it to you?' she asked.

'Don't dodge the question. Are you coming with me to see my mother or not?'

Tonia was flabbergasted. So he was serious. What a man. Why was he so full of himself in that quiet and aggressive manner? Yes, his manner was quiet and very aggressive. That kind of man was dangerous.

'No, Alpha, I am not going to see your mother. You see, I am not husband-hunting. I have just finished school and I am ambitious. I want to go abroad for further studies. I want to do many things, and marriage happens not to be one of them.'

'My mother will come and see you then. I shall bring her tomorrow to see you. You live with your auntie. Never mind what she will say. My mother and I will handle it very well.'

Back home, Alpha talked to his mother. 'Mother, I saw this girl and I liked her. She told me she was not husband-hunting. But there was something about her that I liked so much. You see, since I cannot have Betty, I have to have the next best. And this girl Tonia appealed to me in a way no other girl had. So, mother, bear with me. We shall go and see her. She lives with her auntie. And she would like us to come and see her at her auntie's house.'

'Alpha, my son, I have said that I am no longer going to disgrace myself any more where your marriage is concerned. I have told you that in this

101

world you can marry anybody you like or do not like and still be happy. Didn't you see how happy my marriage was. Your father died young but for his untimely death I would have still been married to him to this day. And it was my own mother who made me marry him. I felt nothing for him, then years later I began to love him and to respect him, and then he died.

'If you want us to see this Tonia, well, all well and good. I am prepared to go and see her and her auntie. But are you sure? Are you perfectly sure that you like her and want to live with her as I lived with your father? Tell me before we go.'

Alpha scratched his head. The expression on his face showed that he was not sure. His mother could read him like a book.

'Well, you see, you are not sure. Betty is married and has two children by her husband, and they live in Lagos. What else can you do? From all accounts, she is happy with her husband, who is an influential man. So, Alpha, you just have to accept it. Accept the fact that Betty can never be yours. So go on and get the next best person for yourself, and forget Betty . . .'

'Mother, do you think I can ever forget her? It is not possible, mother. How could I forget her when she is still alive?'

Alpha's mother began to laugh. 'You children, why don't you understand? Why don't you be realistic?'

'What if Betty's husband dies?'

'Well, it is a possibility. The way death comes these days, yes of course. But you really don't wish Betty's husband ill. You really don't want Betty to be a widow. You . . .'

'Mother, I want Betty to be a widow so I can marry her. Haven't I told you that I cannot really be happy with anyone else?'

'Because of Betty?' Alpha's mother was now angry.

'Yes, because of her.'

'But you are not going to marry her. Get that into your fat head, that you are not going to marry her. If the unexpected happens, that is if her husband dropped dead tomorrow, you would not marry her. This Betty is becoming an obsession, you know. And this garbage must stop, do you hear me? This nonsense must stop.'

Alpha knew when to stop when he got into an argument with his mother. When his father was alive, it was so different. He would sit down in his father's study while they talked about so many things. His relationship with his father was so cordial that even his own mother was a bit envious. Alpha's father had treated him with love and respect. If Alpha wanted anything, it was easy for him to go straight to his father. Most boys would rather go to their mothers first if they wanted something from their father, but not Alpha. And this was because his father made him at ease in his presence and talked to him as he would to an adult. Now his father was dead, and there he was dealing with his mother, who was not as educated as his father, and was also a woman who lacked tact in dealing with her son.

In the real sense of the word, Alpha did not want to be involved in marriage. He was so different from his mates. Yes, he had girls, but he had them only when the sexual urge became unbearable. At this time, all he did was take a woman to his beautiful flat, then send her away when the urge was taken care of. No woman was even allowed to stay the night; no woman was ever allowed to cook for him. Yet he was popular with women because he was so inaccessible. But this popularity must be watched carefully, otherwise the female sex would brand him and make life uncomfortable for him.

Because of his mother's outburst, they did not talk of seeing Tonia's aunt any more, and it was only after a very long time that he met Tonia again, this time in the company of a friend of his. Alpha was the one who started a conversation.

'We did not come after all,' he began.

'Obviously, and we did not expect you. I never told you that you and your mother would be welcome. Such a visit to tell you frankly could be embarrassing.'

'Well, I don't see anything embarrassing about it. I shall merely introduce you as my girlfriend to my mother. That's all. My mother, I am sure, would be glad to meet you, because it would be the first time my mother met a girl I could call my friend.'

Intriguing, thought Tonia. 'I am flattered,' she said aloud.

'You sound as though you don't believe me. It is the truth. Come, let us move to the other side of the bar, it is quieter there.'

Tonia went with him, they sat down and Alpha went on talking. 'I liked you the first day I saw you with your friend. I have been waiting to be sure before I talked to you. I have a lot of problems which I want to share with you . . . Waiter, please come here.'

He asked Tonia what she would like to eat and drink. Tonia burst out laughing. Alpha laughed too. 'No, oh no, I am not going to buy you five chickens. I wanted to impress you and your friend that night, but I guess I made a fool of myself. Please don't misjudge me on account of that . . . Oh waiter, I am sorry, please bring us half a chicken or snails if you have snails, then a soft drink and a bottle of beer.'

When the waiter left, Alpha continued, 'Somehow, I feel like talking to you ever since that night, and now, if you don't mind, I want to talk to you about a certain woman called Betty, who was my childhood love; who, despite the fact that she is married and lives with her husband, still has a great hold on me.'

'Thank you, waiter.' He paid him and went on. Tonia was very still now, and she was a bit disappointed for she had thought that Alpha was going to talk about marriage. 'Go ahead,' she said.

'It's not easy for me, but you see I was a boy of twelve when I met Betty. You would not believe it, but it is true. I was only twelve and Betty was already finishing her secondary school education in Queen of the Rosary, Onitsha. My late sister had taken me to Betty's home to see her mother, who was a very good sempstress. You see the irony of it all was that I missed going to Port Harcourt with my father on that day, and was so upset that my sister was sorry for me and asked me to go with her to Betty's house.

'Betty struck me as a very beautiful girl, and I fell for her immediately. I was only twelve and Betty was my sister's age. Thinking of it now, I wonder how I could have had that kind of feeling for a girl who was ten years my senior. I cannot remember what happened afterwards, but after that day, I went to

Betty's house regularly. I did not feel happy if I did not see her every single day. I began writing her love letters to which she did not reply. When she came on holiday, I would spend all day in her house. Luckily, Betty had a young brother who was about my age, so when I went there, everybody thought I had gone to see Ifeanyi. That was his name. Ifeanyi was my own age, but like my sister, he died early. I think it was Ifeanyi alone who knew that I was in love with Betty. He used to tease me a lot when we played football. Because of Betty, I loved Ifeanyi so dearly that he was like a twin brother to me.

'Then one day, I returned from school and was told that Ifeanyi was ill, and that he had been taken to hospital. I refused to eat and raced to the hospital to see him and be with him. Two days later Ifeanyi died. That was the first death that was close to me. Father hadn't died then. I was thirteen years old, and I could not accept Ifeanyi's death. I refused to eat my mother's food for days. It was Ifeanyi's mother who calmed me down, when my mother could no longer bear my grief.

'When I went to college, Betty was already teaching. I would write her letters and beg her not to reply to them for fear that she would not reply and I would be too disappointed. I would buy her gifts and send them anonymously.

'At school, other boys had girlfriends, but I refused to have one. I confided in one of the boys I thought was my friend, but he let me down so badly that I shied away from school friends. He told everybody that I was in love with a woman who was old enough to be my mother, and that the woman did not even know that I existed.

'I was deeply hurt by his unkind words, and because of this incident, I did not have a very happy college life. I was teased mercilessly by the boys and I had to report to the prefect who dealt with the boys, but my isolation persisted. The boys thought I loved solitude, but I did not. Their unkindness forced me into an isolation which I hated but could do nothing about.

'So I began confiding in my mother, because at that time my father had died. Were he alive, it would have made a world of difference. He would have told me what to do and how to handle my so-called misplaced love.

'I continued writing to Betty. Then one day, I got a letter from her acknowledging all my previous letters. I was on top of the world. My joy knew no bounds. I read the letter over and over again. I carried it in my hip pocket wherever I went. The letter was the first one she had ever written. After a few days, when I had read the letter for the hundredth time, I began to read between the lines and to discover that Betty wrote to me as she would write to Ifeanyi if he were alive. There was no endearment of any kind. Did she not know that I was pining away for her? Did she not know that the boys were teasing me so much that I was in tears?

'No, I must let her know my love for her. I must tell her in no uncertain terms that I loved her and wanted her to be my wife. I was going to tell her that I would worship her for the rest of my life. I would tell her that I would be worthy of her by working very hard and making her rich. I was going to tell her that no woman would ever hold me the way she had done. I would tell her all these things and more, so

107

that she would begin to take me seriously.

'But when I picked up my pen, I discovered that I could not put my thoughts into words. No words were adequate to express my love for Betty. The beginning of the letter was difficult. How was I going to begin the letter? My dear Betty? Betty my love? My darling Betty, the apple of my eye? My only one? My one and only? My sweetheart? My future wife? . . .

'None was adequate. I did not want to be offensive in the beginning of my letter. I should address her simply, my dear Betty. That was enough. Then I would go on and say my piece as briefly as I could, without being misunderstood. For I thought if I made a mistake it would be disastrous for me. I should not make a mistake, lest I frighten her away from me. Now that she had condescended to write to me, I should do nothing that might offend her.

'In the end, I did not write. It was not easy. I thought of her every moment of the day, but I did not write to her. Then one afternoon in school, I received another letter; this time the envelope contained nothing but a passport sized photograph of Betty. I was hysterical, I was in seventh heaven. I had not asked her to send a photograph. Was she falling in love with me? She must be, or why would she send me a photograph of herself? Only loved ones were sent photographs. It was a good gesture, a loving gesture, a timely gesture. Now, I must write, no, not yet, I should reciprocate by sending her my own photograph.

'I looked at my collection, but I did not have a good one. So I decided to go to town and take a snapshot, just a snapshot would do at the moment. If she liked it, I would go to the studio and take a really good one. What was I going to wear? My school uniform? No, that would not do, I did not want to look like a schoolboy. So, if I did not want to look like a schoolboy, I should wear a suit and look as if I had already left school and was working in the secretariat at Enugu.

'But we were not allowed to bring suits to school. Then I must go home and bring a suit, smuggle it into the dormitory, take the photograph and send back the suit. So on a Saturday, I went to the clinic and told a long story to the school nurse, who burst out laughing, patted my back and said, "Alpha and Omega." That was what the boys called me when they teased me. I wondered how the nurse knew. "You have been a good boy. You have never told me fibs. Your story is most interesting. Are you home-sick? Do you want to see your mother?" I nodded, feeling very embarrassed. "Why didn't you tell me?" she said. "You can go home, but make sure you return to the school before six, and get your medicine from your mother." You see, I had told her that I had asthma and I forgot to bring my medicine to school.

'I went home, broke open my box because I could not find my mother who had the key, and took my suit, took a photograph and returned to the school before six.

'That was the beginning. At night I would dream of Betty. Some nights I had wet-dreams. I would wake up and there would be no Betty.'

'Then what happened?' asked Tonia. Alpha became aware of his surroundings again. He was talking to Tonia, who was very kind to listen to his unique love affair. That was the first time he had opened up to talk to another woman about Betty.

'What happened?' asked Tonia again.

'Nothing happened, Tonia. I sent the photographs. After what appeared to be eternity, the photographs were sent back to me. The signature of the sender, I could not read. I suspected that Betty's husband sent them back. I suspected that she might have said something to her husband. But I was not sure. I was in school, still a teenager with a burden, a love burden. Have you ever been afflicted with the burden of love? Can you imagine being in that state when you were not sure what the loved one thought about you? When you were not sure whether she made fun of you, whether she was playing games with you? Or whether she simply pitied you? If you had the misfortune of this experience, then you would understand and appreciate my plight.

'When I could no longer bear my burden, I decided to travel to Lagos, for Betty and her husband lived there. My father had a relative there, so to this relative I went.

'To this relative I went, in my last year in school. Mother protested but I refused to listen to her. Armed with Uncle Ezego's address I went. He was living in Apapa with his family, and was employed as a steward somewhere. Well, he had not quite made it, but he was not yet under. He had a one-room apartment which he shared with his wife and three children. His wife cooked in a corridor, overlooking a gutter which smelt like a corpse. How they survived was a miracle.

'I was profusely welcomed. Uncle Ezego, who left home before I was born, and who had never been home since, welcomed me simply because I was my father's son and therefore his own "brother". He still felt that he belonged even if he had found it impossible because of financial restraints to visit home for over twenty years.

'Tonia, it was not easy to find Betty. How was I to begin? Did my uncle know of our people in Lagos? Yes, of course he knew some of them. So I went with one of his children. There I was lucky to meet a childhood friend living with his parents who saved me from the squalor of my uncle's abode. I moved to their house which was in Igbobi, and two days after we paid a visit to Betty at her husband's place.

'Was she glad to see me? She was not hysterical of course, but I could see that she was very happy in a most refined way. I was so happy to see her. I never thought it would be so easy to find her. My teachers had always said that one succeeded in whatever one wanted to do if one only persevered. I had persevered and had succeeded. I had always believed that Betty had that latent power in her to spur me on to great heights. I knew that with her I was safe from the wicked world, safe from attack, safe as a safe full of money. I had so much confidence in her. I had so much love bottled up. I did want to let her know that I loved, that I cared, that I wanted her to care as well, to uncork this bottled-up love.

'But then she was already married. She belonged to someone else. She had already given her love to that somebody. There was nothing I could do. But then at least I could come to her home and talk to her. Yes, I wanted to talk to her, I wanted to be close to her, to breathe the same air that she was breathing, to tell her that it did not matter that she was married and the mother of two children. I wanted to tell her that I still loved her, that nothing had changed as far as I was concerned.

'She was not looking at me with love as such. There was affection all right, but that was not the kind of affection I wanted. It was the kind of affection one had for one's child or even one's dog. Perhaps I was expecting too much from Betty . . .

'Look, why am I saying all these things to you, Tonia? I am never like this, you know. I rarely confide in anybody. Why am I pouring out my whole life history to you when I have only seen you once or twice? You have a hold on me. Now why don't you talk to me? I have been talking to you about this dream girl of mine who won't let me sleep at night. And you stay there listening and not interrupting me. It is your turn to say something.'

Tonia said nothing and Alpha continued his life history. He went on and on and Tonia was like the wedding guest in 'The Ancient Mariner', listening and not interrupting.

'Betty entertained us well. She gave us food and drinks. She talked politely to us. Then I had the audacity to ask her why my photograph had been returned. She had forgotten. She could not comprehend. Then it dawned on me, perhaps she did not even place me. She had forgotten everything about me. The way she looked when I mentioned the photograph proved that she had never given me a thought at all. And I was pining away for her. I had come to Lagos just to see her.

'When we got back to my friend's house, I cried and the next day I went back to my mother. Soon I did my School Certificate, and went to Lagos to look for a job. I got a good job. I was going to excel in my job. I was going to move mountains to succeed. If I wanted to marry Betty, then I must be good. I must be a Senior Servant. All I wanted was the best for Betty and I.

'Then the disturbances in the country came; there was January 15th, 1966. And overnight night became day and day night. I was the first to flee. My mother simply came to Lagos, packed my bags and took them home. Many returned home, but Betty and her family did not return.

'Miraculously, I survived the war. I was not going to have anything to do with Lagos any more. So I set up my business in Aba. And the other day I saw you with your friend. I did tell my mother about you but we quarrelled because again I brought up Betty and mother was upset. She does not understand. Why not talk to me, Tonia? Perhaps you can help me.'

It took Tonia a very long time to recollect herself. She was shy. How was she going to help Alpha, who was so obsessed with love? He was only in the state of love. He had built and imagined this woman, and was in love with her. The only way he was going to prove his love was by marrying her. That was impossible because the woman in question was already married and was happy in her marriage, or so it seemed.

Alpha said there was a possibility that Betty's husband would die, then he would marry her. He was not planning to kill him? No, he was not going to do anything like that. It was just wishful thinking.

'So your mother was upset?' she finally said.

'Very upset.'

'She had every reason to be upset,' Tonia said. 'But tell me,' she continued, 'have you ever checked

113

Betty up since the war ended?'

'I did once in 1970. I went to the place they used to live, but she was not there, and the neighbours did not know anything about her. I felt they knew but did not want to say anything.'

'You should try again, Alpha. Perhaps you might be lucky, though I don't see how you can win your childhood love.'

'There is no harm in trying, is there?'

'Not at all, no harm whatsoever in trying, except that it is most improbable that you would find her free to marry you. She might have more children by now. And surely you don't want to be saddled with someone else's children, do you, even if the unexpected happened, and this woman agreed to marry you?'

'I have not given the children a thought yet. All I know is that I love Betty and will do everything in my power to marry her one day. I must get her, she must be mine one day.'

Alpha and Tonia developed a very unique friendship, uncommon in Nigeria for those who had no blood relationship of any kind. They saw each other fairly often; when there was a dance, they went together; and sometimes Alpha took her to parties. But though there was no sexual relationship between them, Alpha would not permit Tonia to dance with anybody at these social gatherings. Tonia was greatly amused and did not protest. She was not falling in love with Alpha, but she liked him enormously. When they were together, they talked endlessly on a variety of issues. There was nothing under the sun that they did not talk about, but mostly they talked about Betty.

114

One day, Alpha brought Tonia home to his mother.

'Oh Alpha, is this the girl you wanted me to meet?'

'Yes, mother, Tonia is her name.'

'My daughter, welcome to my son's house. Where do you come from?'

Tonia told her.

'I know your people very well, my daughter. Ikedike and my husband, Alpha's father, traded in palm oil at Okigwe and here in Aba.'

'Mama, Ikedike was my uncle, my mother's brother,' said Tonia.

'You see, Alpha, I know her and her people. I have always said that the world is a very small place. So Ikedike is no more.'

'Yes mama, he died many years ago.'

'That set of men were formidable during their day. They made money quick and died quick. They were really the men in their time. Alpha's father and your uncle maintained a very good relationship, my daughter. They worked hard, drank like fish, ate as if their meals were their last and died young in their prime. They did everything to excess. There was no control. Both of them could sit down and drink a whole bottle of whiskey before a meal, and after the meal, continue with dry gin. They when they finished, they went in search of women, other men's wives and . . .'

'Mother, please spare us the details.'

Tonia laughed. All mothers were the same. She was sure that her own mother would talk exactly like Alpha's mother was talking. 'Mama, don't mind Alpha. I know that what you are saying is true. My own mother told me worst stories about my father when he was a young man. You mothers were wonderful in those days. We of the younger generation would not tolerate what you tolerated.'

'Thank you, my daughter. Here,' and she gave her some of the things she brought from home.

Tonia thanked Alpha's mother and left.

'Alpha,' his mother called. 'I heard some rather unusual news last week.' Alpha was all ears. 'I heard that Betty is now back in Lagos and that she lost her husband.'

Alpha's mother was crafty. She had heard the news some weeks ago, and did not quite know how she was going to break it to her son. She thought that now Betty was in Lagos and free to remarry if she wished, Alpha would make up his mind either way.

She knew that there was no point talking to her son about marrying someone else if he did not receive a refusal from his childish love, Betty. Unknown to Alpha, his mother had worked very hard to locate Betty in Lagos, and she had believed and was to be proved right, that Alpha, on knowing of Betty's widowhood, would race to Lagos. She had planned it all and it was working according to plan.

So Alpha travelled to Lagos as soon as he was able to. It was not difficult to locate Betty, who was now an executive in an insurance company in Lagos. While he was away, his mother invited Tonia home and told her she wanted her to be her son's wife. If she was willing, when Alpha returned from Lagos, they were going to perform all the customary obligations. As experienced as Alpha's mother was, she knew that Alpha's love for Betty was not mature. Betty had been too remote and inaccessible and this had sharpened Alpha's boyish yearnings. Marriage between the two would never work. Both were different in many ways, both had different backgrounds, different values and their friends had nothing in common.

Tonia was a good girl and she knew where she came from. She would do for her son. Tonia wanted to think it over. She had her ambition which was to have a university degree, any other thing was secondary, including marriage. But that did not stop Alpha's mother. She told Tonia that she could continue her education if she wanted. She knew her son was not going to stop her from reaching any height in her education.

When Alpha returned from Lagos he went straight to Tonia. He had had a raw deal in Lagos. He spent four hours at the airport; the taxi driver who took him to a hotel in Surulere charged him ten naira instead of the normal five naira. He had to spend three hours on Ikorodu Road because of a 'go slow', and by the time he arrived at the hotel he was half-dead.

He checked into the hotel after depositing a hundred naira and he was given a room where the air-conditioner was not working, and just as he was about to change into his pyjamas and fall asleep, though he was hungry and wanted to eat, "NEPA took away the light" and he was in darkness.

But the management said they had a generating set, and they would soon switch it on. He waited for half an hour but nothing happened, so he lit a candle that he saw in his room and went downstairs to find out why the hotel was still in darkness. He was told by the receptionist that the generating set was out of order and had gone for repairs. He was too tired to

117

be angry so he went to bed, tired and hungry. In the morning, he went down for breakfast, sat down and read the menu. At least there was coffee. If he was unable to eat anything, perhaps coffee would be all right. When the steward brought the orange juice, he declined it because he was not sure that the water used in diluting it was boiled. As for the bread, it was too dry and stale and the butter on the menu turned out to be margarine.

'Please can I have coffee?' he asked the steward. He brought the coffee but it was already cold. What was there to eat? He called the steward again and said, 'Can you get me hot coffee, please?'

'Oga, de cook don go, no hot water for make coffee.'

'Be a Nigerian man,' someone behind Alpha said. And they laughed in spite of everything. The steward of course heard and brought Alpha a pot of hot coffee. Alpha had never welcomed a cup of coffee as he did that one given to him by the steward. He thanked him profusely and left one naira under the plate.

He hailed a taxi soon after and went to Betty's office. But he was told that it was too early, that Betty normally came to the office around ten o'clock. It was only nine o'clock and Alpha hated waiting. He could keep people waiting for hours on end, but nobody dared keep him waiting. What was he to do? Perhaps he would go back to the hotel, check out and return to Betty's office. As things were moving, he would have to go back to Aba that day.

But he did not reckon with the unpredictable Lagos traffic. By the time he returned to Betty's office, it was already noon. He was in her office for about half an hour, thanked her and took a taxi back to the airport.

'Tonia,' Alpha said, 'for the best part of my childhood and adult life, I have loved a shadow. I did not know the real Betty. The Betty I saw in Lagos was not the woman of my imagination. I saw a strange and sophisticated woman in her early forties. Life had not been too kind to this woman. She had changed beyond recognition. Then I wondered, was I the one who had changed or Betty? Who was this Betty that I fell for in my boyish years? What was she like? What sort of person was she? Was she a good woman or a bad woman? What were her likes and dislikes? What had happened to her in the years of her marriage? Who was her husband who had died during the war? He was not from our own home so I knew next to nothing about him and what he did for a living.'

'Were you well received?' asked Tonia. Alpha hesitated before he replied.

'Yes and no. She was strange and aloof. She remembered me all right, asked her secretary to make coffee for me, and such rituals, then . . .'

'Then what?' asked Tonia.

'Then someone came in. Perhaps he was a colleague of hers, or perhaps he was her boyfriend, for she was now no longer married, having lost her husband. They talked in such an affected manner that I was thoroughly disgusted and . . .'

'And,' added Tonia, 'you did not receive the kind of attention you wanted, that you expected, that . . .'

'How did you know?' asked Alpha in surprise.

'Go on, what happened after the coffee?'

Alpha was silent. He was not talking again. Why,

119

he had wasted precious time loving a shadow, punishing himself unnecessarily. Oh, but he should have known that the Betty he knew was the Betty he created for himself. He should have known that that kind of love affair was uncommon; that Betty had had more experience of life than he; that her friends obviously could never be his friends as well; that he was out of place, that he did not fit into Betty's life; that his mother was right in saying that his love for Betty was an obsession and that he would get over it.

Then he was aware of Tonia's presence and he went on, 'I will never visit Lagos again.'

'Because Betty ignored you?' asked Tonia.

'She not only ignored me, Tonia, she made me look small and stupid in the presence of her colleague or boyfriend, whichever he was. I was treated almost like a poor relation who had come to look for a job in Lagos. I was angry. I did not touch the coffee which her secretary had brought. I held my temper, and Tonia, you know my temper. I held it until the man left the office. Then I told her I was leaving. I was visiting Lagos and I thought I should say hello to her . . .

' "Oh, that was nice. Oh, aren't you drinking your coffee?" she said. "No, thank you," I replied. It was not what she said but how she said it that was offensive. She had that kind of affectation all "been tos" have. "Bye then," she said.

'She did not even ask me personal questions to show that she recognised me. She did not ask when I would be going back to Aba, nor did she ask about home people, not to mention my mother. I was hurt. I left her office. I stood in the street for more than an hour waiting for a taxi that would take me to the airport. Taxis zoomed past me without stopping to pick me up. It was after I had been there for a while that some good Samaritan asked me where I was going. I told him. He told me to cross the road, take a turning to the right and there hail a taxi for the airport. I was charged fifteen naira. I jumped in, swearing that I would never visit Lagos again.'

Alpha paused. There was again an awkward silence. Then he began, 'Can I take you to see my mother this weekend?'

'With pleasure,' said Tonia.

OTHER BOOKS BY THE AUTHOR

Efuru
Idu
This is Lagos & Other Stories
Never Again
One is Enough